Death in the Choir

by

Lorraine V. Murray

Lorraine V Murray

TUMBLAR HOUSE
'Bona Tempora Volvant'

Arcadia
MMIX

Printed in the United States of America

ISBN 978-0-9791600-7-3

This is a work of fiction. All of the characters, organizations, places, and events portrayed in this novel are either products of the author's imagination or are used fictitiously. Any resemblance to any persons, living or dead, is purely coincidental.

Visit our Web site at www.tumblarhouse.com

Cover illustration and design by Jef Murray
(www.JefMurray.com)

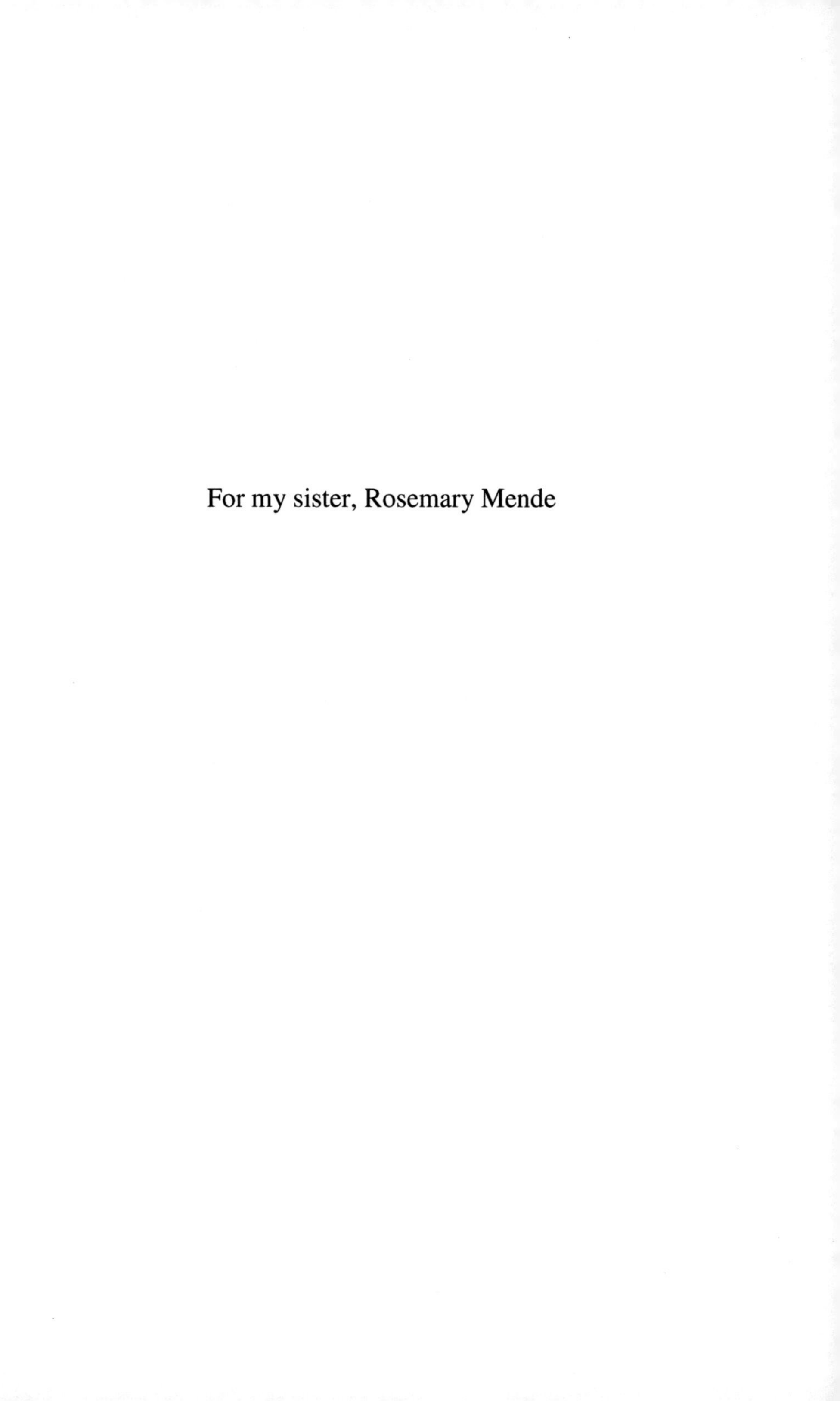

For my sister, Rosemary Mende

Chapter 1

The sound was ungodly – and it was coming from the soprano section, as usual. *Patricia is definitely on the edge tonight*, thought Francesca Bibbo. *Sounds like she's calling the cows home.* The stream of tortured notes continued until the choir director, Randall Ivy, a tall man in his late forties and impeccably dressed in a pristine white shirt and beige slacks, slammed his hand down on top of the organ. The angry sound reverberated throughout St. Rita's Catholic Church.

St. Rita's was located in the heart of Decatur, Georgia, a town of about 16,000 people just a cat's whisker away from Atlanta. Despite its proximity to the big city, Decatur remained a heavily wooded area with somewhat of a small-town atmosphere. Residents weren't that surprised when raccoons and possums wandered into their backyards looking for handouts, and there were occasional sightings of red-tailed hawks swimming through the sky.

The church, along with a rectory, convent, and school, was situated on five acres near the town square. St. Rita's had a stunning interior with glossy oak pews and stained-glass windows that glowed like jewels. In the afternoons, the sun radiated through the glass to paint colorful images on the floor. Unlike many newer Catholic churches that had banished kneelers and statues, St. Rita's was more traditional.

Parishioners still got down on their knees to pray and could frame their prayers by gazing on a towering marble statue of Mary in the front left of the church or St. Joseph on the right. But, as was fitting with Church doctrine, the marble crucifix occupied the highest point over the altar. Francesca Bibbo, an uncertain alto, often glanced at the crucifix during choir practice and shaped a silent prayer, especially when things started going awry, as they were now.

"No, for heaven's sakes, no!" Randall Ivy fumed. His well-tanned face was now a dangerous shade of red, and as he ran his fingers through his blonde hair, Francesca noticed little furry horns appearing on his scalp.

"*Someone* in the soprano section is flat *and* loud, a deadly combination."

Five of the six sopranos cast uneasy glances at each other, while the sixth one, Patricia Noble, stared at her glossy fingernails, looking unconcerned. All the other choir members seemed to know who the offending party was, despite an unwritten law that the director didn't use names when correcting the singers, all of whom were volunteers.

The choir consisted of 20 parishioners ranging in age from 25 to 80. The group sat at the back of St. Rita's near the organ on Sunday mornings, a fortunate arrangement in Francesca's opinion, since this meant the congregation couldn't stare at the singers during Mass.

She was somewhat self-conscious about singing in the first place, and she dreaded being the center of attention. Besides, it was just as well that the parishioners couldn't see Randall, she reflected, because he often looked like he might explode from rage when choir members hit the wrong notes. During rehearsals, he tried to contain himself, usually issuing a general warning to the entire choir in his efforts to shame the perpetrator.

Patricia, a curvy bleached blonde of 40, was a bit of a special case, however. As he continued berating the soprano section for errors, she went on studying her pointy red nails as if testing them for sharpness. Flawlessly dressed, the five-foot-ten-inch Patricia was reputed to have taken her ex-husband to the cleaners and now devoted her life to shopping.

Francesca shifted uncomfortably in her chair. Thirty-eight and widowed for two years, she admitted to herself that she had ulterior motives for joining the choir. Her voice on the very best of days was only average, but she was tired of living alone in the house that she'd shared with her husband. She was ready to start dating, but dreaded facing the dreary bar scene. And the choir seemed as likely a place as any to meet a man.

Last month she had attended her first meeting of the "Feisty Forties," St. Rita's singles group for parishioners, but it had been woefully disappointing, since ten women and only four men had shown up. One of the men had a terminal case of bad breath, two seemed to be exceptionally heavy drinkers, and the fourth had prefaced too many statements with "as my mother always says."

Still, she didn't want to be cruel. She was aware that her standards were impossibly high, because her husband, Dean, had been both a friend and a sweetheart, a rare combination. Also, as she found herself telling friends now and again, repeating something her aunt had said long ago, she herself was no "spring chicken," so who was she to be casting the first stone?

Sitting at home alone wasn't good for her; that was certain. Father John, the pastor, was always urging parishioners to get involved in various ministries, running the gamut from helping at homeless shelters to visiting the sick and homebound, and when he had described singing in the choir as a ministry to the congregation, she had decided to try that.

Maybe the choir would work out. There was the slightly balding, somewhat introverted Gavin Stewart, who was a widower. He sometimes toted a small taciturn son with him to rehearsals, and Francesca, who had no children, at times fantasized that she would become a mother to someone else's child late in life. She would finally have someone call her by that beautiful term "Mom."

Then there was Thomas White, a short, well-built man whose outstanding feature was turquoise-blue eyes. He was a real music buff who often shared musical scores with Randall. A bachelor, Thomas sometimes showed up at church with a girlfriend, but since he never brought a date to choir parties, Francesca suspected the relationship was probably quite casual.

The choir director himself was somewhat of a mystery. Randall Ivy had sandy-blonde hair and an athletic build with skin that turned the color of pale honey in the sun. His yellow-green eyes reminded her of a cat. In her estimation, he was very handsome. He had been the director for about three years, and she knew little of his past. Rumor had it that Randall was gay, but Francesca wasn't so sure.

Usually she could detect the telltale signs immediately, but his sexual identity seemed somewhat murky. Sometimes, when he smiled at her, his catlike eyes lightly flickering over her figure in a distinctly heterosexual fashion, she had the definite impression he was interested. Other times, when he was flailing his arms directing a piece of choral music, he looked foppish, although Francesca imagined it would be impossible for even a linebacker to appear anything but effeminate in similar circumstances.

"Let's give it another try," Randall said. "And remember the enunciation. It's not foreverrr," he growled, rolling his r's in a particularly grating fashion. "It's fah-evah. And it's not spirrrit, it's spihdit. Remember, in choral music, r's are ugly."

"Spihdit sounds like 'spit it,'" Rebecca Goodman muttered under her breath to Francesca. A plump, friendly woman who sat to Francesca's left and described herself as "fortyish," Rebecca was the lead alto and had a strong, beautiful voice.

Randall returned to the organ and began pounding out the opening notes to "If Ye Love Me." By the end of the first measure, Patricia's sour notes had filled the sanctuary faster than smoke from burning incense. And r's were peppering the air like gnats at a South Georgia picnic. The blood rose in Randall's face once again. He retracted his fingers from the organ as if the keys were on fire.

"Sopranos, step up to the organ," he snarled. "Everyone else, take a break."

Francesca genuflected as she faced the tabernacle on the altar before heading out the back door into the vestibule. She often wondered what God Himself must think as He surveyed this motley crew, trying their hardest to churn out decent music for the congregation. It was hard to tell if the people in the pews cared one way or the other. Sometimes, when the choir fell flat on its face, someone would stop by the organ to congratulate Randall for a stunning performance. Other times, when the notes flowed as sweetly as maple syrup, no one said a word. As for God, He remained stubbornly silent on the issue.

The men had gathered in the vestibule and were discussing the latest football scores. Francesca yearned to join in, but she kept her distance because she rarely even knew which teams were playing. Usually, if anyone mentioned basketball, football or baseball to her, she had a standard reply. "When it comes to sports, I have an advanced case of attention deficit syndrome."

Tonight she decided to stick with the other altos, since it was too much of an effort to pretend she found touchdowns fascinating. *Besides,* she thought, *I'm not looking my best.* She had spent the day answering the phone in St. Rita's rectory, and she'd arrived home late with barely enough time to grab a sandwich and feed Tubs, her 10-year-old arthritic cat, before heading to choir practice.

There'd been no time to scrub off the day's make-up and reapply a fresh coat, so she felt grubby and unappealing. To make matters worse, she could feel a blemish doing its best to blossom on her chin. *Despite my mature age,* she reflected dismally, *my skin persists in believing I'm still an adolescent.*

"Do you think he's gay?"

Francesca was shaken from her self-deprecating thoughts by the question Rebecca Goodman had whispered to Shirley Evans, the youngest choir member. Shirley, 25, had an upturned nose and a round face haloed with auburn curls. She also had been blessed with a curvaceous figure that she showed to best advantage in snug jeans and sweaters. Francesca was often grateful to God that Shirley was married and the mother of a fetching two-year-old girl.

Who needs more competition in the dating department? she thought, edging her way closer to the two women to join their discussion.

In the background Randall could be heard pounding the top of the organ and emoting loudly, "No, ladies, you hold that note for two beats, not one. And I don't want to hear those r's! Let's try it again."

Shirley giggled and a few of the men looked her way longingly before returning to their discussion of a particularly memorable touchdown.

"I think he probably is," she said.

"What makes you think so?" Francesca asked.

"Well, just look at the way he plays the organ. Isn't it obvious?"

"I don't know," Rebecca chimed in, "sometimes I get the feeling he's looking at me – and he's not always staring into my eyes, if you know what I mean."

Shirley and Francesca laughed in unison. Just then, the door to the vestibule opened, and Randall rushed out. Was it Francesca's imagination or was he looking directly at her? And he had the nicest yellow-green eyes.

"OK, everyone, let's try the whole piece from the top one more time."

The men and women filed back into the church and took their places.

"And if anyone says 'spirrrret,'" Randall warned, seating himself at the organ, "I will personally excommunicate them."

"I didn't know choir directors had that power," commented Andy Dull, an older man in the bass section.

"The pope has given me a dispensation."

This time the singing went well. Evidently Randall had said something to silence the shrill flat notes that were Patricia's calling card, and all the other sopranos were singing at top lung power in an apparent attempt to drown out any possible errors on her part.

"OK, it's a wrap," Randall said finally. "Thank you all for coming tonight. See you on Sunday."

Francesca picked up her music and her purse and was about to leave the church when she heard Randall call her name.

"Mrs. Bibbo, will you stay after for a moment or two?"

Be still my beating heart, she thought, as Shirley and Rebecca cast her amused looks. "Be sure to give us a full report," Rebecca whispered, gathering up her music. "See you tomorrow night."

One by one, the choir members drifted out into the brisk November night. Now it was just Francesca and

Randall. As he gathered up his sheet music from the organ bench and headed toward her, she mentally began reciting a familiar litany of self-recriminations.

Why didn't I take the time to apply a fresh coat of war paint? Why did I wear this baggy sweatshirt? And why did I gain two pounds last week when I was trying to lose five?

Francesca, who was only five foot three, had to diet furiously to keep the extra pounds at bay. As a chubby child she'd been taunted by her classmates and had developed a mental picture of herself as obese. She knew it wasn't healthy to compare herself to the grinning skeletal figures gracing the front of women's magazines, but she often did it anyway.

She'd inherited her olive complexion and molasses-brown hair and eyes from her parents, who had died when she was in her twenties. Her father's family had originated in Sicily, and her mother's in Naples. She had also inherited a longish, decidedly Italian-style nose, the bane of her existence. Her husband, Dean, had thought her nose was cute, but in her estimation it was too prominent, especially in a culture that seemed to idolize women with smaller models.

Her stream of thoughts suddenly ran dry as Randall sat down next to her. She gave him her best smile, unconsciously running her tongue over her front teeth to give them an extra shine.

"How are you tonight, Mrs. Bibbo?" His catlike eyes swept over her face in a slightly seductive way.

"Oh, please, call me Francesca." She was horrified to feel blood coursing into her cheeks. *I can't believe I'm blushing like a teen-ager,* she groaned inwardly. "I'm a little tired from answering phones at the rectory, but other than that..."

"How long has it been since you left your job at Krenshaw State University?"

"Let's see, it's been two years now." She winced as an image of a gargoyle suddenly darted through her mind. *My ex-boss,* she thought grimly.

"What did you do there?" He sat down beside her and leaned in just a bit with a look of real attention on his face.

"I worked in the publications office for nearly ten years. At first, I really loved it, especially my first boss." He nodded in an encouraging way, so Francesca went on.

"She was from Alabama and used the most wonderfully picturesque expressions. She'd say, 'It's like pushing a rope' to describe how hard it was to get some people to finish projects on time. And when deadlines were looming, she'd tell us 'We're getting our tails in a crack.'"

Here she paused, delighted to see that he was laughing. "I think I know what your boss meant," he said. "Sometimes I feel like I'm definitely pushing a rope with the sopranos."

Now he glanced at her hand. *Is he looking for a wedding band?* She wondered.

"So, Francesca, why did you leave that job?"

"Well, my wonderful boss retired, and the one who took her place was…well…let's say she was impossible. After that, it was easy to leave."

He smiled again, as if he really understood her. *What a nice smile*, she thought, *I don't think I've ever seen whiter teeth – and so straight. Which reminds me, I wonder if he's...*

"And since then, how have you kept busy?"

She reflected on her laundry list of volunteer activities. She and Dean had lived frugally, and he had invested their savings wisely, so now she didn't have to work, as long as she continued watching her pennies. Of course, she'd be willing to work in that dreary office 24 hours a day if she could only have her darling husband back again.

"Oh, this and that. My husband died, and…" She was surprised at how shaky her voice sounded. He looked at her with compassion in his eyes, and it took her a moment to compose herself.

"I'm very sorry to hear about your husband."

"Yes, well, it was quite sudden. An accident." She had to change the subject or she would start crying.

"But to answer your question, I do a little volunteer work at the rectory, lots of reading, some gardening, you know..."

Randall moved closer to her now. "Well, there's something I wanted to ask you."

She could feel his body heat radiating toward her and caught a whiff of heady and very masculine cologne. He was so close she could see how cleanly he shaved and how carefully starched his shirt was. *Do other women find men's Adam's apples sensuous? Not those big bulbous ones, of course, but there's definitely some appeal in a well-formed apple like his.*

"Yes?" She suddenly felt very shy. At this close distance he was no doubt noticing every single flaw of her complexion, and there were quite a few, the result of a lifelong battle with acne.

"Would you be interested in being my choir assistant?"

"Your what?" The words flew out of her mouth before she had a chance to think. *I must sound like a babbling fool*, she thought. *He probably thinks I don't know the meaning of the word.*

"I'm looking for someone to buy sheet music, organize it, keep an updated list of phone numbers and e-mail addresses for choir members, print programs for special concerts, send out e-mails about rehearsals -- a lot of little tasks I'm handling myself now. And you'd be paid, of course."

A little extra money for Christmas certainly couldn't hurt, she thought. *And as his assistant I could work closely with him and get to know him better.*

"Well, what do you say?"

He has dimples. How strange that I didn't notice them before.

"It sounds interesting – and I could use some extra Christmas money." She felt her cheeks growing warmer as two completely unexpected images suddenly flashed through her mind out of nowhere: the two of them, wrapped in a delicious embrace; the two of them, standing before the altar to take their vows.

She began stuffing her sheet music into her folder to avoid his eyes. "When do I start?"

"I'll give you a call later in the week and we can get together. I have your phone number on the choir list."

Now Randall seemed very officious as he stood up. "Unfortunately, the pay isn't fabulous, but it's dictated by the pastor, as is everything else."

He looked pained, but he didn't really have to go into the details with her. Everyone in the choir was well aware of the long history of misunderstandings that existed between the pastor and the last three choir directors. Father John Riley had been at the helm for seven years, and he was well-loved by the congregation for his upbeat sermons and dry wit. But he had a definite temper, and sometimes the people who worked closely with him felt its sting.

The last choir director, enraged by the pastor's meddling in the day-to-day details of the choir, had stormed out of the church one day during the early morning Mass, never returning. He had gone on to become a world-renowned organist, and there were still days when people in the choir would reminisce about the quality of the musical selections he had chosen.

There had been a mad scramble to replace him, and Randall had been hired. Although she knew most people thought he didn't have the same skill set as his predecessor, he was known for working hard to select traditional music and for keeping the choir motivated. Now history seemed to be repeating itself with the pastor.

"You probably know this beastly thing is on its last legs." Randall straightened up a stack of hymnals while shooting the aged organ a dark look.

"One of these days it's going to die a foul death right during Mass. Of course, I've told Father John innumerable times, but he doesn't want to spend the money to buy a new one, so we have to keep adding patches here and there. I swear I'm tempted to sneak into church late one night and put the thing out of its misery by hacking it to death with an axe."

He gave her another of his disarming smiles, dimples and all.

"Well, enough of my problems. We'd better call it a night. I'll get in touch with you soon."

Picking up her music folder and her purse, Francesca genuflected in the direction of the tabernacle. For just a moment, her eyes glanced lovingly at the serene statue of St. Joseph, her favorite saint. She loved the Blessed Virgin Mary dearly, but there was something about St. Joseph that intrigued her.

She wished there were a prayer like the "Hail Mary" to honor the man who surely had helped Mary give birth to the Christ Child in that lonely stable in Bethlehem. She had always pictured Joseph as being the first to hold the babe and look into His eyes.

Now, as she opened the back door of the church vestibule to step outside, she saw a dark figure coming up the steps. Although Decatur was relatively safe, there was always the chance of a street person coming up to ask for money, and they made her nervous when she was alone. Startled and suddenly fearful, she pulled her purse toward her and drew back. Then she realized it was the pastor, and greeted him warmly.

"How are you tonight, Father John?"

The priest's dark hair was in disarray, standing up in tufts around his ears. Once again, she thought of horns.

"Just fine, my dear, and you?"

She smiled in response. *I wonder if he remembers my name*. She'd been a parishioner for six years, but it was a very large congregation and he wasn't good with names. Now she watched as Father John Riley opened the door to the church, genuflected, and went in. It was then that she realized she had forgotten to light a votive candle for her husband, as she did every week after rehearsal. She quietly returned to the front of the church, lit the candle, and then kneeled down to pray. But as the conversation at the back of the church started heating up, she had trouble concentrating.

"I'm concerned the organ is going to break down during our Christmas Eve performance," she heard Randall say. "It's really on its last legs."

She heard the pastor's reply. "We have to be good stewards of the congregation's money. I can't see spending thousands and thousands on an organ when there are so many other needs."

She completed her prayers and stood up, hurrying quickly down the aisle and out the back door. The two men were so engrossed in conversation that neither one seemed to notice her.

Randall's voice was rising. "Father, what do I have to do to make my point about this ungodly piece of junk? Sacrifice myself by committing Hari Kari right here on top of it?"

She was already out of the church, so she didn't hear Father John's reply.

Chapter 2

As Dean's snoring reached a crescendo, Francesca awoke with a start. She sleepily glanced over at the bedside clock – eight a.m. Then she stretched her hand out to stroke Dean's hair. He had the loveliest thick hair, the color of semisweet chocolate, with little gray patches she loved to tease him about.

She was just about to whisper, "Dean, stop snoring!" as she had done a hundred times before, but as her hand touched the pillow, she came to full consciousness. There was no one there. Dean had been dead two years and still she could be tricked by memory into believing he was sleeping beside her.

Rivulets of hot tears coursed down her cheeks and turned cold as they trickled into her ears. *I'm not going to start the day this way. I just can't. The mourning period is over. Dean would want me to get on with my life.* It was the familiar litany she'd recited ever since receiving the phone call two years ago telling her that her husband had been killed in a car accident on his way home from work. They had just celebrated their 15th wedding anniversary.

She had met Dean at the University of Florida in Gainesville, when she was majoring in philosophy and he was studying mathematics. She had dated a series of men who were intent on avoiding commitment, and had been extremely wary when this good-looking, intelligent man had shown up in her life. He seemed too good to be true.

On their first date, they had talked for hours, and Francesca had found herself stunned by how much they shared in common. Like her, he had been a fat child; like her, he had been raised by a school-teacher mom. Best of all, he was eager to get married and start a family.

After they married, he went on to get a graduate degree in computer science and then landed a well-paying job. Francesca had soon discovered that a philosophy degree wasn't worth much in the marketplace, so she had reluctantly entered the public relations field. He had been born in Gainesville, and she had grown up in Miami, and they had yearned to live in Florida after graduation, but Dean's career had brought them to Georgia.

She had been raised a strict Catholic in a household that traced its Italian Catholic roots for many generations back. Still, when she went to college and majored in philosophy with a minor in psychology, she suddenly found all her beliefs challenged and shaken. Before long, she had become what the nuns had warned her about: a fallen-away Catholic. Dean had been baptized in the Methodist church, but had little interest in religion, at least in the early years of their marriage.

Then, one day, out of the blue, Francesca surprised herself and everyone who knew her by returning to the Catholic Church. She told her friends that something – someone? – had been tugging at her, and she had given in to that strong, mysterious impulse.

Much to her delight, Dean had expressed interest in learning about the Church, and had persevered through nearly a year of instruction before being confirmed during an Easter vigil at St. Rita's. It had touched her deeply that he had taken Joseph as his confirmation name, since he knew Joseph was her favorite saint.

Rubbing her eyes, she sat up and looked toward the foot of the bed, where something warm and furry was pressed against her legs. It was Tubs. *He was the one snoring*, she thought. Pure white except for a tail with raccoon stripes and a black patch on his back shaped like Africa, the old fellow had taken up residence in her bed shortly after Dean's death. And she had not had the heart to insist that he sleep in his cat bed in the hall.

When she leaned down and petted Tubs tenderly on his head, the slanted green eyes opened and the snoring transformed itself into a deep, rumbling purr. She didn't quite trust people who complained that cats were aloof. It seemed to her that cats mirrored their owners' emotions. She cherished Tubs, and he lavishly returned her love by dissolving into ecstatic fits of purring whenever he saw her.

"Hey, Tubs." She scratched lightly behind the raggedy ears. "It's time to get up."

Because Tubs' arthritis was so bad, it was hard for him to leap from the bed, so she picked him up and deposited him gently on the floor. He made a beeline for the kitchen and stood expectantly by his food bowl, meowing like a lost kitten. After she had quickly brushed her teeth and washed her face, she poured a generous helping of dry food into his bowl. But he just stood there, gazing at her hopefully, so she shrugged and opened a can of wet food, his favorite smelly concoction. She mixed everything together and placed the bowl back on the floor.

The phone rang precisely at 8:45. Heading into the living room, she heard the faint sounds of gobbling emanating from the kitchen.

"Hello?" she said cautiously. If she heard a suspicious click and then a tentative "Mrs. Bibbo?" she'd know it was a salesperson -- and she usually hung up at that point.

But it was a familiar voice. "Hey, I hope it's not too early to call," Rebecca Goodman said.

"Not at all. I've been up for a while. You alright?"

"Oh, yeah, everything's fine." Rebecca dropped her volume a bit. She was taking a break from the fifth-grade class she taught at St. Rita's school.

"I can't talk long. The little darlings are watching a film about retroviruses. I just wanted to check with you about our Choir Chicks' meeting. Are we still on for seven tonight?"

"Seven it is."

A few months ago, Francesca had invited three other women from the choir – Rebecca Goodman, Shirley Evans, and Molly Flowers – to her home for drinks and snacks. The tenors had jokingly dubbed the gathering the "Choir Chicks" -- and the title seemed to stick. Despite being a male, Tubs had been designated the president, and he was the eager recipient of cheese tidbits at the meetings.

"I'm going to try a new quiche recipe," Rebecca enthused. "It's made with non-fat cheese and a non-fat milk substitute, so it shouldn't be too fattening."

"Sounds good," Francesca said automatically, although she had an aversion to non-fat products. It was probably because her mom had used them so liberally when she was growing up in a futile effort to help her lose weight.

"So how did last night go?" Rebecca's voice was dripping with curiosity.

"Oh, you mean the talk with Randall? Well, nothing to report yet. He just asked me to be his choir assistant."

"His assistant." Rebecca's voice feigned a husky sexiness. "Woo, girl! What are you going to assist him with?"

"Oh, you know, really sexy things like buying sheet music and organizing it."

Suddenly there was the sound of screaming and thuds at the other end of the line.

"Oops, I have to go," Rebecca interjected. "The natives are getting restless. See you tonight!"

While Tubs began a long, involved process of washing his face and ears, Francesca brewed a pot of coffee and sat at the dining room table, gazing out the window. It was a truly smashing day in Chelsea Heights, the very hilly area in Decatur where Francesca lived.

The oaks and maples were dressed festively in their fall regalia of orange, yellow, and red. A robin was sipping water from the birdbath out front, and a squirrel was dragging along a piece of stale biscuit that she'd put outside yesterday.

It's so beautiful, she thought, just a little sadly. No matter how much she tried to banish them from her mind, it seemed every season brought memories of Dean flooding back in.

It had not been a perfect marriage, far from it. They had definitely locked horns on a number of issues. But they had been good friends, and she missed the comfortable intimacy they had shared. She could tell him every fear, insecurity, doubt, and worry that plagued her. He had been a really good listener and had a way of reassuring her, no matter how anxious she had been: “Don’t worry. Everything will be fine.” Somehow, when he said it, she believed it.

“Alright,” she announced to Tubs. “No blues for me today.”

Tubs paused from his whisker washing to stare at her meaningfully. She noticed he had licked his bowl to a high gloss, and she knew he was probably pining for seconds.

“You want more?”

He gave a little meow, and she obediently ladled more food into his bowl. It was true that he was overweight, and some people might put a cat like him on a diet. However, she felt that he deserved a few pleasures, and the vet, who was overweight herself, had never suggested that his eating habits were unhealthy.

Francesca poured herself a bowl of cereal and a second cup of coffee, and then resumed her spot by the window, where she could do some serious neighbor-watching. At that moment, the train gave a loud hoot as it approached the crossing on Coventry Road three blocks away, and a chorus of neighborhood dogs let loose with some mournful howls.

She saw the young mother across the street, dressed in a trendy business suit and pointy heels, strapping her wailing three-month-old baby in his car seat. She knew the little guy was being dropped off at a daycare center while the mom went to work. *Even tiny kids are on nine-to-five schedules these days. I know it's not politically correct, but I think daycare is a shame.* She'd been the child of a working mom and could still remember how she had resented babysitters, especially a particularly grouchy one named Mrs. Snapper.

Since she and Dean had not had children themselves, his death had left her all alone in their three-bedroom house. Well-meaning friends had advised her to sell it and had also encouraged her to keep her job at the university. "Being busy will be good for you" was the usual advice. But she loved their home, and the idea of selling it was very unsettling. After all, Dean had left his imprint everywhere, in the hardwood floors and ceiling fans he'd added, and in the grape vines he had planted outside. And after so many years of being imprisoned in an office, quitting her job had given her as much joy as she imagined Lazarus surely experienced when he was called back from the grave.

Some mornings she volunteered to answer phones in St. Rita's rectory, and other days she visited elderly shut-ins. She also kept up the vegetable garden in their front yard and tended roses in the side yard. She didn't miss the frantic pace of the workplace. She loved taking her time in the mornings and not having to join the huge stream of cars heading to work on the crowded highways.

The phone rang an hour later. This time she let the answering machine pick up the call.

"Good morning, Francesca, it's Randall. Are you there?"

She nearly tripped over Tubs in her rush to pick up the phone.

"Randall, how are you?" She was suddenly deeply grateful that she wasn't living in the future, when phones would no doubt come equipped with video screens. She wouldn't want Randall to see her in her baggy pajamas patterned in a black-and-white Guernsey-cow print.

"Just fine. I'm a few miles from your house. I know this is short notice, but would it be alright if I dropped by?"

"Give me fifteen minutes to get dressed. I'll put some more coffee on, too."

"I'll give you twenty. See you soon."

While Tubs stared at her in what she thought of as feline disbelief, she sprinted through the living room, gathering up magazines, two apple cores, a pile of clean laundry, and three half-empty coffee cups. Next she ran into the bathroom and stripped off her pajamas. Deodorant, bath powder, bra, panties, jeans, and sweater. A little eye make-up and foundation, a touch of lipstick. She quickly gathered her hair up into a pony tail. Five minutes to go. Back into the kitchen she ran, nearly flattening Tubs, to prepare a fresh pot of coffee.

When the doorbell rang, the scent of coffee was filling the house. She'd had time to put on her little pearl earrings and the slightest touch of cologne. She hoped he would think this was how she always looked each morning. Opening the door, she was pleasantly surprised by how dapper Randall seemed. Impeccably dressed and with every golden hair in place, he was carrying his brief case in one hand and a bakery box in the other.

"Good morning! You look lovely." Then he handed her the box. "A few pastries from that new French bakery in the Square."

Francesca thanked him and led him into the dining room. She peered into the box of assorted croissants and muffins, noting with approval the delicate buttery smudges on the waxed paper.

"There goes my diet," she joked.

"You don't need to diet. You're fine as you are." He sat down at the dining room table, placing the briefcase near him on the floor.

Even if he's lying, I'll take the compliment. She put down placemats and napkins, poured them each a cup of coffee, and arranged the croissants and muffins on a platter. Meanwhile, Tubs had positioned himself beneath the table near Randall's feet, and he was gazing up at him.

"Nice cat," Randall said absently, touching Tubs' head. But for some reason, Tubs shrank back, his fur puffing out ominously.

"That's strange." Francesca took a sip of coffee and then selected a croissant from the platter. "He's usually a lot friendlier."

Helping himself to a croissant, Randall picked up a napkin to dab at the corners of his mouth.

"Wonderful coffee, but I can't stay long. I'm on my way to my other job."

"What do you do?"

"Well, as much as I'd like to devote myself full-time to music, the pay at the church is rather abysmal, so I have to wear another hat – a very dull one, I'm afraid. I'm a CPA."

"Ah, but that means you probably can balance your checkbook, which is more than I can do," she laughed.

There was a moment of silence as they both sipped their coffee.

"Not to change the subject, but I overheard some of your discussion with Father John last night, although you were still talking with him when I left. How did it turn out?"

"Hopeless, I'm afraid. The man just won't listen to reason."

As he took another good-sized bite from a cream-cheese croissant, she noticed how much he seemed to relish his food. She felt herself blushing as an uninvited image danced through her mind: She and Randall feeding each other chunks of wedding cake, laughing as they licked frosting off each other's fingers.

"Unless the organ has a complete breakdown and is declared officially dead, Father John refuses to come up with the money for a new one." Randall polished off the croissant and reached for another one.

Her mouth full, she made a small sympathetic murmur. *Thank God he can't read my mind,* she thought, feeling ashamed of her romantic impulses.

"Father John had the audacity to suggest that I start looking around for possible donors to raise money for a new organ. Can you imagine?"

Francesca blinked. It did seem rather unlikely that a choir director would also be expected to be a fundraiser. But the parish had some very wealthy members. It was possible that Father John saw Randall as someone likely to get their financial support.

"I'm sure you can do it, though," she said enthusiastically.

Randall just smiled. "I have to confess I have an ulterior motive to my visit this morning. I'd like to leave you a list of the sheet music to purchase during the next few months. You can get the money to cover the purchases from the church secretary." He hesitated. "That is, if you're still interested in being my assistant."

The sunlight glinted off his blonde hair in a most interesting way. *His skin is flawless,* she thought somewhat enviously. *And he has such nice big shoulders.*

"So are you?"

"Oh, yes, I'm still interested." *Boy, am I ever*, she thought, and could feel more blood flooding into her face. *He probably thinks I have the flu or something.*

"I'll leave you the list and the key to my office." He snapped open the briefcase on the floor beside him. "But I have to warn you: It's a real mess in there. When you look up 'pack rat' in the dictionary, you'll see my picture."

He handed her the key and the list. "Just keep track of your time, and you'll be paid at the end of the month." He frowned now. "Oh, yes, is $12 an hour too pitiful? That was Father John's best offer."

"It's fine, really. After all, it's not rocket science. More coffee?"

He checked his watch. "I wish I could, but I have to get to work. But would you like to have dinner with me tomorrow night?"

She hesitated. It was the old instinct of a married woman, she realized. *Well, here it is, my first date in two years.*

"I'd love to."

"I'll pick you up at seven. We'll go to the new Italian restaurant on the square -- if that sounds good to you?"

"Perfect."

Tubs had been lurking quietly beneath the table and chose that precise moment to make his move. With an unusual spryness, the old cat lunged for Randall's ankle, took a quick nip, and then withdrew into the corner of the room.

"Oh, my gosh!" Francesca nearly overturned her cup. "He's never done anything like that before. Bad cat, Tubs! Randall, are you OK?"

Randall bent over and surveyed the damage. Francesca noted with horror that the slacks looked expensive and brand-new.

"Don't worry," he said evenly, although his eyes had an angry glint. "Just a small rip in the fabric. No blood."

He stood up and picked up his briefcase. "Thanks for the coffee, Francesca. And I'm glad you've agreed to help me out with the choir. I think we'll work well together."

Was it her imagination or did he give her an especially meaningful look as he said that? *You need a reality check,* she told herself ruefully. *You're imagining things.* After Randall left, she polished off another croissant, promising herself she'd walk an extra mile that afternoon to work it off. Tubs, evidently pleased with himself for his successful attack on the intruder, begged for a saucer of cream.

Here I am rewarding misdeeds, she thought as she heeded his wishes. *I'd be a terrible mom.*

After lunch, she began preparing a tray of brownies for the Choir Chicks' meeting. She followed a newspaper recipe that promised to produce the deadliest, richest, moistest dessert ever. *And I'm not substituting any of that non-fat stuff for the high-test either,* she vowed, as she put the butter and chocolate in the microwave. Even though she watched her weight obsessively, she'd learned that it was better to allow herself occasional high-fat treats than to eat the fat-free stuff, which only stimulated her sweet tooth.

The day went quickly. She dashed to the grocery store to stock up on wine for the meeting and pick up more food for Tubs. Pausing at the cosmetics section, she couldn't resist buying two lipsticks for her dinner with Randall. She had to smile at the flowery titles: "Purple Passion" and "Exquisite Embrace."

Well, I guess they wouldn't sell many products if they were called "Lifetime Commitment," but that's what I'm longing for.

And then she saw the image of Dean's face in her mind, and she whispered a little prayer for him.

* * *

Rebecca Goodman arrived at seven sharp. She was carrying a shriveled-up quiche that reminded Francesca of a museum artifact, although she would never in a million years share her opinion with her friend, who was very hesitant about trying new recipes.

"I'm afraid it doesn't look much like the picture in the magazine." Rebecca placed the quiche on the cocktail table in the living room. Then, giving Francesca a quick peck on the cheek, she plopped down on the couch.

"Look, before the rest of the gang arrives, I have something to tell you."

Francesca poured each of them a glass of Chardonnay and then sat in the rocking chair opposite Rebecca. "I'm all ears."

"Well, two things. First of all, you probably won't be too thrilled to hear this, but somehow Patricia's invited herself to tonight's meeting."

Francesca winced and took a sip of her wine. Sadly, Patricia had an overblown ego and enjoyed flaunting her wealthy lifestyle. She wasn't popular in the choir where she fancied herself the lead soprano, despite all evidence to the contrary.

Still, I know Jesus loves her, and I should be kinder to her, Francesca thought. *Didn't He say, "Love one another as I have loved you?"*

"Well, we'll make the best of it, I suppose," Francesca replied. *I'm going to avoid being rude to her, I really am,* she promised God mentally.

"The other piece of information is quite juicy, and I wanted to tell you before Patricia gets here." Rebecca took a sip of wine and picked Tubs up from the floor, where he had been looking longingly at her.

"Rumor has it that Father John has enlisted Randall to drum up a big sum of money to cover the cost of a new organ. He refuses to take the money out of the usual church coffers."

Rebecca paused for dramatic effect, while settling the old cat on her lap.

"The best part is that Randall evidently dropped by Patricia's house last night after choir practice. He's acting very interested in her – at least to hear her tell it. But I suspect our choir director is no fool. I think he's after Patricia's money."

Francesca's spirits sagged. *I hope Randall doesn't think I'm a wealthy widow with money to burn.* Then she glanced around the living room, which was furnished with a faded rug and a 20-year old couch, its fabric patched in numerous places. *I probably have nothing to worry about.*

Now she felt confused. She didn't want to broadcast the news that Randall had asked her out, but she also hated to hide the truth from Rebecca, who had been a good friend to her after Dean's death. *Oh, the heck with it, everyone will know soon enough anyway.*

"Guess what? Our choir director asked yours truly to dinner tomorrow night."

Rebecca's eyes widened. "Oh, I, uh," she stuttered. "That's wonderful." She looked embarrassed. "I certainly didn't mean to imply he's only after women's money..."

Francesca got up from the chair impulsively to give her friend a quick hug. "I know you didn't. And, don't worry, if he tries to get me to write a check, you can bet it'll be our very last date!"

The doorbell rang. It was Shirley Evans, her cheeks a plum color from the chilly evening, carrying a fruit-and-cheese tray and a bottle of Merlot. She was wearing white corduroy pants and a big fluffy yellow sweatshirt. After putting the tray on the table and handing the wine to Francesca, she took a moment to pet Tubs, ensconced on Rebecca's lap. Then she gave Francesca and Rebecca quick kisses and settled on the couch.

"Red or white wine?" Francesca asked.

"Whatever's open."

Francesca was pouring a glass of Chardonnay for Shirley just as the doorbell rang again. Glancing outside, she spotted a glistening white Mercedes parked in the driveway behind her somewhat ancient Honda.

"Let me get that for you." Shirley jumped up from the couch. As she opened the front door, she let out a little startled cry. Coming up behind Shirley, Francesca could see Patricia Noble, perfectly made up and dressed to the nines in a black silky sweater, black pants, and leather boots. Her hair framed her face in some flawless, expensive haircut.

"Patricia, I uh..." Shirley looked at Francesca for further instructions.

"Patricia is joining us tonight, isn't that nice?" Francesca announced. "Come on in, Patricia, and make yourself at home."

Patricia bustled in, carrying a large Saran-wrapped covered tray of lavish-looking hors d'oeuvres. "I bought these at the new gourmet shop downtown. I hate to be bothered with any kind of kitchen duty, if you know what I mean."

Sitting down in the rocking chair Francesca had just vacated, Patricia glanced at Tubs, who seemed to return her gaze inscrutably.

"What's the cat's name?"

"Tubs," Francesca said.

"I'm not much of a cat person." Patricia paused to adjust one of her earrings while looking at him in a clinical way. At that precise moment, Tubs launched an enthusiastic flea hunt on his back. "They seem so cold and distant."

Francesca didn't say a word as she poured Patricia a glass of wine. Much to her chagrin, Tubs now managed to leap gracelessly from the couch, so he could show off for company. Pulling a dirty, chewed sock filled with catnip from beneath the coffee table, he began shoving his face into it like a drug addict. Rebecca and Shirley giggled at his performance, while Patricia gazed around the room as if she were surveying the "before" photo in a home-renovation magazine.

This time the doorbell didn't ring. Molly Flowers simply pushed open the partially ajar door and made her entrance. Nearly 50, Molly was a cradle Catholic like the rest of the group, but she prided herself on being what she called "progressive." A staunch feminist, she was constantly railing about the Church's policies on celibacy and women in the priesthood, and she often annoyed the other, more traditional members of the group.

However, Molly was the kind of person who would do anything for a friend, so the other women put up with her diatribes. A nurse in labor and delivery, she had a voice that revealed her roots in Destin, Florida. As she was fond of reminding the group, it was also called "The Redneck Riviera" because so many Southerners vacationed there. Placing a bowl of salsa and a tray of chips on the table,

Molly did what appeared to be an exaggerated double take when she saw Patricia.

"Well, fancy seein' you here!"

"I'd meant to join this group sooner, but I've been too busy until tonight." Patricia speared an hors d'oeuvre.

"Doin' a lot of shoppin' these days, Patricia?" Molly seemed to be enjoying herself.

"Yes, as a matter of fact, I spent the entire day at Phipps."

Of course, it would be Phipps, Francesca groaned inwardly. It was one of Atlanta's trendier malls, made popular by the city's many wealthy residents who apparently had discovered life's ultimate meaning in recreational shopping.

Molly opened another bottle of wine and poured herself a glass.

"I need this." She settled down on a cushion on the hearth. "I've had quite the day. We delivered five babies in a row."

"I know what you mean." Patricia was examining her wine glass, and Francesca hoped it didn't have any smudges on it. "I spent nearly three hours this afternoon trying to find a purse to match this outfit." She tenderly caressed a small velvet bag dangling from her arm as if it were a sacred relic.

"Well, we all have our crosses to bear," Molly drawled, offering Tubs a crumb of cheese, which he wolfed down greedily.

As the women started helping themselves to the array of food on the coffee table, Francesca reminded them that freshly baked brownies awaited them for dessert.

"Oh, none for me, I'm dieting." Patricia's voice had a whiney edge.

"What on earth for?" Molly exclaimed. "Sugar, you look like a good wind might blow you over."

"Well, if you must know, I've gained two pounds this year and I don't want to keep on gaining." She looked meaningfully at the plump Rebecca, who was filling her plate with finger sandwiches. "It's so easy to just let oneself go."

Patricia chewed on a grape and took a small sip of wine. "And you know when you have a new man in your life, well…"

All the munching sounds came to a dead halt. Romantic news was always considered an excellent topic of conversation at Choir Chicks' meetings.

"Do tell," said Shirley. "Anyone we know?"

"As a matter of fact, yes. Randall and I had a late dinner last night. It was very nice. We went to that new Italian restaurant in the Square."

What a fool I am, Francesca thought sadly. *Randall probably has a bevy of women he takes to the same restaurant. The waitresses no doubt have a good laugh whenever he comes in with a new one.*

"Well, what's he like on a date?" Molly prodded.

"Very cultured, very much a gentleman." Patricia paused to adjust a gold link on her charm bracelet. A wave of her perfume wafted across the room. *Expensive,* thought Francesca.

"So, is it serious?" Rebecca cast a knowing look at Francesca.

"Oh, it's too early to tell." Patricia dabbed her carefully painted lips with a napkin. "We had a lovely time, but that was it. We didn't, er, well, there was nothing..." Her voice trailed off delicately.

"So he didn't put the moves on you, huh?" Molly leaned in to re-fill her plate.

Patricia looked pained. "No, of course not. But I did get a chance to tell him that I expect to have a solo now and again. After all, I've been taking voice lessons for the past five years."

"And?" prompted Shirley. "Did he agree?"

"Yes, he did. He said he felt that someone of my musical caliber deserves more recognition." Patricia impaled a piece of kiwi fruit on her toothpick. "He plans to give me a solo for Christmas Eve."

Francesca didn't dare look at the other women. She suspected they might be on the verge of a major giggling attack. *I bet he's buttering up Patricia for a contribution to the organ fund.*

Patricia brushed one of Tubs' stray hairs from her skirt. "He said something rather perplexing though."

The other women gave her their full attention.

"He was pretty steamed about Father John. He said that if Father continued showing him so much disrespect, he might just walk out and let Father handle the Christmas Eve music. But that's not all."

The room was silent except for the sound of Tubs purring as he gnawed on the catnip sock.

"Evidently they had quite a blow up recently. And Randall told me that if Father John doesn't change his attitude, he might not be pastor of St. Rita's much longer."

"What on earth would make him say that?" Molly hiked her eyebrows up so far her forehead seemed to vanish.

Patricia blotted her lips delicately with her napkin. "Randall wants to get the parishioners to sign a petition complaining about Father John. He wants to send it to the Archbishop."

"What would anyone complain about?" Rebecca's face mirrored the surprise of the other women.

"He told me there's a group that wants the church renovated. But Father John thinks it's a waste of money, so he's been dragging his feet. And Randall also said there are some people who feel Father John should do something about Father William's homilies."

Francesca sighed. *Dear Father William,* she thought. He was the young associate pastor of St. Rita's, and she liked him very much. However, he had inadvertently made a reputation for himself by delivering sermons that invoked the wrath of a huge number of parishioners on a regular basis.

"Well, I wouldn't sign any petition," Molly said firmly. "That's over the edge."

"I agree." Patricia sipped her wine. "I think Father John is very nice and quite competent." Then she fingered a gold filigree earring in one of her pink, seashell-shaped ears. "And rather sexy."

Chapter 3

Father John Riley groaned as he glanced at the clock on the bedside table. Five a.m. and it was dark outside, and all he could think about was having a cigarette. The craving welled up in him with the force of a demon.

Now I know how it must feel to be possessed, he thought. *Maybe I should call in an exorcist.*

Ever since the doctor had told him to stop smoking, Father John's spirits had been spiraling downward. He'd managed to survive a whole week but then had broken down and sneaked a smoke yesterday morning. It had been delicious, but the guilt he felt afterwards made him wonder if it'd been worth it.

If a man can't have sex, he reflected sourly, *at least allow him to smoke himself to death. Doctors shouldn't be allowed to banish any simple pleasures from the lives of celibates. Sex. Oh, no, why did I even bring the word to consciousness? Now I'll be pursued all day by images of voluptuous women striking lurid poses.*

He had entered the priesthood late, at age 45, after a series of failed relationships with women. In his twenties, he'd felt keenly drawn to the priesthood, but the notion of living without a woman had seemed an insurmountable obstacle. He had wanted a wife and family, and he couldn't imagine himself living alone. But, as he'd neared 40, he'd faced the facts. The chances of finding a wife and having a family were growing increasingly dim, while his attraction to the priesthood seemed to be gaining steam.

He knew that he was generally considered good-looking, maybe because he had a full head of black hair and dark green eyes. He'd had no problems attracting women in his twenties and thirties, but had been unable actually to sustain a romantic relationship. It was always the same scenario. The woman would demand more and more of his time, and he would find himself withdrawing. He needed a certain amount of solitude to keep his sanity. There would be recriminations, tearful accusations, and finally the inevitable break-up.

He sighed. The irony was that now that he was a priest, everyone demanded his time. But of course it was different because he didn't have to succumb to the emotional roller-coaster ride of romantic relationships. Plus, he was doing the work the Lord had called him to. But what he hadn't realized, until he started wearing the white collar, was that women who would never have given him a second glance when he was a layman now found him attractive beyond belief. And there seemed to be some unspoken rule that spurred some women to hug and kiss priests until the poor men were driven to distraction.

These same women, who'd never have dreamt of revealing the intimate details of their sex lives to, say, their medical doctor or even their best friend, also felt compelled to unload themselves to him in the confessional. One parishioner in particular came to mind because he had been unprepared to defend himself the first time she confessed.

"Bless me, Father, for I have sinned," she began in a breathy voice. Then, before he could stop her, she had launched into a truly lascivious stream of details about her sex life that made him cringe with embarrassment. When she next showed up, he was ready to interrupt her the moment she began her description: "And then he pulled me closer and wrapped his arms around me, and…"

"Just a moment, my dear." He cleared his throat to stall for time. "There's really no need to give all the details of your sins. Just a general, uh, sense of what is involved is fine."

This anonymous woman came to confession about twice monthly. She always hid behind the privacy screen, so he couldn't see her face, and she seemed to be struggling primarily with the sins of the flesh. He thought of her privately as Lady Chatterly.

If it weren't for sex, he thought darkly, *the confessional would be filled with cobwebs.* In his estimation, one of the seven deadly sins – lust -- was getting far too much air time in the 21st century. *Envy, pride, gluttony, sloth, anger, and despair have just about been forgotten.*

Suddenly, the image of a cigarette with a beautifully glowing red tip loomed in Father John's mind. His mouth was dry and tasted vile. Wondering if there might be a forgotten cigarette in the drawer of his bedside table, he hopefully rummaged through the pencils, coins, and holy cards. But he'd been very thorough with his earlier search-and-destroy mission. He started saying a "Hail, Mary," which always calmed him.

Then he sat up in bed with a start. There was someone

– or something – in the hall right outside his door. A loud scratching sound assailed his ears, making him suddenly recall the rumor that had long circulated at St. Rita's church. The rectory was said to be haunted. Supposedly the ghost of the church's first pastor paced the halls now and again, although Father John had never encountered him, and certainly didn't believe in ghosts. "The poor old pastor was probably so worked to death in life," Father John was fond of saying, "that he wouldn't allow himself the luxury of full retirement even after death."

The scratching sound stopped as suddenly as it had begun, and Father John picked up his rosary beads. As he began praying, his mind strayed. He loved the priesthood, but sometimes he fantasized about cloning himself. With the number of Catholic priests dwindling to an alarmingly small number, a pastor's list of duties could be overwhelming. There were funerals, weddings, and baptisms, in addition to visiting the sick and hearing confessions. Many parishioners were of the opinion that if the Vatican would just change the celibacy requirement, the priesthood would again flourish. But he disagreed. It seemed to him that the worldly lure of having a well-paying job with all the trimmings might play a bigger part in keeping men out of God's vineyard than the celibacy rule.

The vineyard. That reminds me: I'm also supposed to cut down on my drinking. Either that or find a new doctor.

The scratching noise started up again. Whatever it was, it was drawing nearer and nearer to his room. Suddenly the image of a drooling satanic being, complete with horns and hoofs, galloped into his mind. He was sure he detected a sudden chill in the room, even though the heat was on full force.

He continued praying the rosary, and soon the noise stopped. It would be just his luck to be visited by an apparition of the devil, when thousands of others in the nearby town of Conyers were claiming they'd seen the Blessed Virgin Mary. And since sites where Mary was presumed to have appeared tended to attract millions of religious seekers a year, he had to wonder: Would a site rumored to be darkened by the presence of the Evil One attract hordes of perverse pilgrims?

The door to his room now shuddered, and the scrabbling noise grew louder. Silence emanated from the assistant pastor's room down the hall. Father John realized he'd have to deal with the situation himself. *That's the way it always is,* he reflected bitterly. *If there's a dragon, get the pastor to slay* it.

"Lord Jesus Christ, Son of the living God, have mercy on me," he prayed, while crossing himself and reaching for the crucifix next to the alarm clock. Next he grabbed his bathrobe from the floor and wrapped it around him.

"May the forces of Heaven prevail against the powers of darkness," he implored, throwing open the door.

A black blur leapt at him, nearly knocking him to the floor. He caught himself just in time, sinking down on his knees. He shut his eyes as his face was covered with moisture and a rank odor filled the room. *Time to face the demon,* he thought. Still clutching the crucifix, he opened his eyes.

"Spot!"

The big drooling mongrel was sitting inches away from him, expelling clouds of bad breath into his face. "You're supposed to stay downstairs. How in blazes did you get up here?"

The ungainly mutt had shown up about a week ago on the rectory steps with a small nametag dangling from his leather collar. The word "Spot" was engraved on the tag, although the animal was solid black. Spot was still teething and, judging by the hunk of wood lying on the carpet inches from his gaping mouth, he had recently ripped off a piece of molding to munch on. Spot panted, his tail wagging joyfully.

"Bad dog, Spot! You know you're not supposed to chew on the walls."

But then the humor of the situation struck him as he lay back on the floor with Spot's face inches away and the dog's wet nose glistening in the morning light. As the priest started laughing, Spot eagerly nosed him under the chin. Father John stood up and brushed bits of dust from his clothing.

"Let's get you some breakfast, boy. It is going to take divine inspiration to find a way to stop you from eating the rectory, piece by piece."

As he started downstairs, Father John heard the sounds of the computer keyboard emanating from the assistant pastor's room. *William's getting an early start on his homily*. Then he blanched. "*Homily,*" he thought crossly, *it sounds so frilly. Why can't we just say "sermon" like we used to?* It was hard for him to swallow all the changes the Church had gone through in the 1960s. *After all, Christ didn't give the "Homily on the Mount."*

The clicking sounds sped up. *William must be on a roll. I just hope this week's gem doesn't alienate as many people as last week.*

He was fond of Father William Snortland, who was 30 and a newly ordained priest. Father John knew the young man rose in the dark each day to work on sermons that would be, in the young priest's estimation, inspiring, educational, and reflective. He was a pudgy, balding man with a trusting expression that matched his childlike faith. And he was known at St. Rita's for responding with deep love and compassion to the sick and dying. Father John sighed again. There was really only one big problem. According to many parishioners, sermons were Father William's Achilles' heel.

Although Father William dutifully spent hours in preparation, he somehow managed to annoy the majority of his listeners when he stood up to preach. One Sunday, Father William had mentioned that animals definitely didn't go to heaven. His statement had prompted a flurry of e-mails to Father John from all the animal lovers in the parish. Another time, he had suggested that spending too much time at the gym could be a sign of vanity, and therefore a sin. The joggers, bicyclists, and weight lifters had headed to their computers that time.

* * *

Down the hall, Father William yawned widely. Today he was outlining the various ways that parishioners could prepare themselves for Christmas. *There are far too many parties during Advent,* he reflected. *People should wait to celebrate on Christmas Day.*

As he deleted a few lines, and then inserted a nice quote from St. Augustine, he glanced across the room, where he was met by a pair of dark-brown beady eyes. His hamster, Ignatius, had been running on the wheel most of the night and now seemed ready for a treat. Father William reached into a nearby bag of sunflower seeds and handed a few to the little animal, who sequestered them in his cheeks for later.

The wheel, that's it! he thought. *I'll mention the wheel of the liturgical year and the relationship between Advent and Lent.*

* * *

In the kitchen downstairs, with Spot watching his every move, Father John started the coffee and threw two pieces of bread into the toaster. It was too early for the cook to show up, and he was glad. He needed some time to pray in silence. As the scent of coffee started to fill the room, his craving for a cigarette skyrocketed. He opened a can of food for Spot, and then sat down at the rather rickety kitchen table, where he read morning prayers from a small, well-worn book.

"Come let us worship the Lord with joy." As he poured himself a cup of coffee, he heard strains of organ music drifting over from the church.

Barely six o'clock. Randall's also getting an early start today.

He frowned. It hadn't been easy telling Randall there

was no money to buy a new organ. But he'd learned over the years that if he said "yes" to every parishioner's request, St. Rita's would soon be bankrupt.

* * *

An hour later, Randall was still at the organ. Music was the only thing that blocked out his troubles. He had come to St. Rita's eager to bring dignified, beautiful music to the congregation. It wasn't just altruism; music kept him from dying of boredom in his accounting job.

"Call to Remembrance" could be a really beautiful piece of choral music, he reflected, *if the choir just had the manpower to pull it off.*

"Remember not the sins and offenses of my youth," he sang under his breath. In his estimation, the problem with an all-volunteer choir was that only some of the members could sing worth a damn. He'd tried his best to shame away the lousy singers with very broad and sarcastic hints, but it didn't always work. He stopped playing. *How am I going to rein in Patricia? Why did I promise her that solo at Christmas?*

At the time, he recalled, he'd hoped to get a start-up donation toward the organ fund. Surely that would be worth it. Maybe it looked like he was compromising his principles, but he was doing it for the good of the whole congregation. At that moment, as if on cue, the organ let out a bleat that he privately thought of as its dying moose call. Frustrated, he jiggled a few of the stops and tried the measure again.

Better this time, he thought, *but who knows when it will happen again*?

Absently, he reached into his shirt pocket and extracted a white pill. For his nerves, the doctor had said, and to keep anxiety and depression at bay. He picked up the cup of water nearby. He usually had trouble swallowing pills, but he had cut this one in half earlier, so it went down easily.

* * *

A few miles away, Francesca was dismally surveying the contents of her closet.

Why in the world did I agree to a date? I'm really not ready. Oh, aren't you, answered another voice in her head, *then why did you join the choir in the first place? Wasn't it to meet men?*

She sometimes wondered if everyone had a series of voices in their heads that seemed to hold conversations of their own. Whenever she read about saints heeding the voice of God, she wondered how they could tell which voice it was. She pulled out a purple sweater and a black skirt from the closet. With some silver earrings and a silver necklace, she'd look fine. *Keep it simple,* she reminded herself. And maybe if she skipped lunch, she'd feel less guilty about eating Italian food tonight.

Sitting in the Italian restaurant that evening, Francesca wondered why she had gone to such trouble. She had dressed carefully, surveying herself countless times in her full-length mirror and wishing for the millionth time that she weighed less. She had also applied a coat of "Purple

Passion" lipstick, chuckling again at the name.

The restaurant was cozy enough with tiny tables lit by candles and swathed in snowy linen cloths, but at first Randall seemed ill at ease.

Maybe he really isn't interested in women, she worried *– or he's trying to butter me up for a contribution to the organ fund – or both. Oh, why can't I just relax and enjoy myself?*

As they began eating their appetizers, Randall, much to her relief, never broached the topic of money. And after he had poured them each a glass of wine, he started to relax. He looked at her earnestly.

"You know, I sometimes wonder if I'm totally insane, spending as much time as I do on the music for St. Rita's. I mean, do you think people really care whether they sing one of the grand old hymns like 'Holy God, We Praise Thy Name' or something like 'We Are Many Parts' by whatshisname…that Marty guy?"

She laughed. "I think I remember singing that one at a church I went to in Florida. Doesn't it have lyrics that go, 'We are many parts. We are all one body?'"

"That's it! That's the very tune." Now he began to sing, and she joined in: "May the Spirit of love make us one indeed."

He took a sip of wine. "It's revolting, but very popular. Songs like that are making big money, even though they're incredibly trite. And, frankly, they remind me of some of the hippie stuff from the sixties!"

He paused to refill their glasses from the carafe on the table. *He comes to life when he talks about music,* she thought. *He's really fun.* But when the entrees arrived, he ate silently, looking pensive. She downed three glasses of Chianti and ate every bite of manicotti. Once their plates were removed, he cleared his throat in a particularly officious way. And then, much to her horror, he extracted a sheet of paper from his pocket and handed it to her.

"These are my ideas for the organ fund-raising drive. What do you think? Would this letter inspire someone to contribute?"

She looked the letter over quickly. *He's outlined the costs and explained the benefits*, she thought. *He's certainly made it look like a worthy cause.*

"Well done," she smiled, and he brightened considerably. Then there was a long pause as the waitress brought desserts. At the precise moment that her fork shattered the tender shell of the cannolli, he leaned a bit closer to her.

"Would my words inspire you personally to, uh, contribute?"

She dabbed at her lips with the linen napkin. "I, er, think so. If I had the money, that is…"

"That's good to know." Now he folded his dinner napkin carefully by his plate. "Look, don't get the wrong idea. I just wanted your advice on the letter; I'm not hitting you up for money. And to tell you the truth, I really hate going after money at all. But I want the music at Mass to be really good -- and that organ…" His voice trailed off.

"Please, Randall, you don't have to explain. I think what you're doing – trying to raise money —which I know you hate – well, it's rather noble in a way."

He raised his eyebrows in an exaggerated double-take.

"Noble? What on earth do you mean?"

She could feel the blood warming her cheeks. *Am I making a total fool of myself here?* But she had to tell him how she felt.

"You're doing it for the good of the congregation. You're doing it so the music at Mass will be the best quality. So…I guess I see that as noble."

He smiled at her. "Listen, don't nominate me for sainthood. Let's face it: I have some selfish motives here. Every choir director wants the latest and greatest instruments."

"More coffee?" The waitress' tone of voice indicated dread. Francesca glanced around and realized she and Randall were the only diners left. The waitress clearly wanted to go home.

"No, thanks," Randall said. "Just the bill will be fine."

They drove in silence back to her house. As he parked the car, she asked, "Do you want to come in for another cup of coffee or an after-dinner drink?"

"That sounds wonderful, it really does, but I have to get up early tomorrow to get ready for Mass."

Oh, Lord, I hope I don't look too disappointed. It's not that I want a relationship with him, but I would love to feel attractive – and desirable – again. The other voice chimed in quickly: *Shut up! Don't make this into a big dramatic event. He turned down coffee, not a marriage proposal.*

"OK, well maybe another time." As she began fumbling with her seatbelt, he leaned across the seat and undid it for her. Then he quickly took her in his arms and planted a long, succulent kiss on her lips.

Her heart started beating so quickly she was sure he could hear the knocking sounds. The voices in her head were suddenly silenced. Drawing back, he gently traced the outline of her lips with his finger.

"You're a beautiful woman, Francesca. And I'll definitely take a rain check on that coffee."

"Thank you. And, yes, we'll have to…uh…yes, you can have a rain check." She got out of the car quickly, surprised at the intensity of her reaction. He walked her to the door, and this time she kept her distance from him, bidding him a quick goodnight and then scurrying inside.

As she locked the door behind her, she realized that she felt guilty. *I still think of myself as married.* Then she went to the kitchen for a glass of water and saw Tubs sitting by his bowl, staring at her. She gave him a generous supper and headed to bed. Her last thought as she fell asleep that night was: *Definitely not gay.*

The next morning she arrived at St. Rita's promptly at 9:30, since the choir always spent a half hour before the 10 a.m. Mass rehearsing the day's psalm and the anthem. This morning she was particularly curious to see how Randall might react. Would he act warmly toward her, would he ignore her – or pretend nothing had happened? And she wondered if she'd be able to look at him without blushing.

There was no choir rehearsal room at St. Rita's, so the group rehearsed in the back of the church. As Francesca headed for her assigned seat in the alto section, the first person she saw was Patricia, who was draped over the organ with an almost possessive look in her eyes as she gazed at Randall.

She's wearing a rather low-cut blouse for church, Francesca noted darkly. And then she remembered her earlier resolution to be kinder to Patricia. *I'm going to have to start with my thoughts.*

"You look lovely this morning," she heard Randall say to Patricia and then Patricia giggled and seemed to puff up like a peacock. Francesca was surprised to feel a hot tide of jealousy surge from somewhere deep within her and settle in her throat.

"Good morning, Randall, good morning, Patricia," she said as nonchalantly as she could. Patricia barely looked at her, but Randall smiled.

She took her seat next to Bertha Chumley, an obese cheery woman in her sixties whose clothes always seemed to need a more thorough washing. Today, she noticed, Bertha was abloom in an expansive flowery print dress with ruffles on the bodice and a skirt that looked like it might provide shelter for a small town. Once again, Francesca realized she was giving hospitality to unkind thoughts. *Lord,* she prayed, *save me from my judgmental mind.*

Bertha looked at Francesca appraisingly. "Are you coming down with something? You've got a rash."

A rash! Francesca fumbled in her purse for her mirror and scrutinized herself frantically. Her face was covered in bright red splotches. Hives, something she had once been stricken with in college. When she'd left the house, there had been no sign. She quickly hurried downstairs to the ladies room, where she splashed her face with cold water and added a generous layer of foundation.

While she was making her repairs, she heard someone

talking out in the hall. The word “archbishop” floated through the door. Curious, she inched toward the door and stood listening. There was a small group gathered in the hall, talking about signing a petition to send to the archbishop.

“We’ve put up with these problems long enough,” one man said angrily.

Randall’s a fast worker, she thought, heading back upstairs. As she stepped into the sanctuary, she saw Father John being engulfed by a female parishioner. The woman planted a firm kiss on his cheek, leaving a scarlet imprint, and then squeezed his bicep appraisingly.

“Oh, he’s such a darling priest,” the woman gushed to a friend standing nearby.

Father John, whose face had turned the color of rare roast beef, nodded vaguely and then stuck his hand out to greet the next parishioner.

“Let’s go over the psalm. Number 652 in your books,” Randall announced, as Francesca took her seat between Bertha and Rebecca.

“My soul pines for you like a dry, weary land without water,” she read silently from the book. “On my bed at night I remember you.” *Hmmm, rather a nice sentiment*, she thought, glancing up at Randall, who seemed deeply engrossed in directing the men.

“Guys, let’s speed it up a little,” he urged, as the tenors and basses sang through the first verse. “This is not a dirge. Let’s put some joy into it.”

After the women practiced the psalm, it was time to run through the day’s anthem. There were only about ten minutes until Mass started, and Randall seemed nervous.

There never was enough time on Sunday mornings.

"Come on, folks, get out your music and get ready to sing."

The choir members all stood up. "What are we singing?" Bertha began shuffling through a nest of sheet music that she'd stuffed into an over-sized floral-print canvas sack.

Randall took a deep breath before replying. "The same thing we practiced at rehearsal this past Thursday: 'If Ye Love Me.'"

As Bertha continued shuffling, he glanced meaningfully at his watch. "Everyone should have a copy," he said through gritted teeth. Bertha continued riffling through her bag.

"I wasn't here, and I don't have the music either," came a nervous voice from the tenor section.

With a dramatic sigh, Randall flipped through a folder and found extra copies of the music.

"OK, folks, let's give it a try." He plunked out the opening notes on the organ.

Suddenly Father John appeared at the choir director's side. Francesca noticed that Randall's eyes had a hunted look now. The priest fidgeted with a page in his hymnal.

"Look, I don't want the 'Lamb of God' sung in Latin today. Do it in English like the other churches in the archdiocese. The congregation won't sing if it's in Latin."

Randall didn't say a word, but Francesca saw the muscles in his cheeks clenching. He had commented time and again to the choir that St. Rita's parishioners refused to sing, no matter what language the songs were in. They enjoyed sitting snugly in their pews and listening to the choir.

"Right, Father," he said quietly, and the priest rushed away. Randall again pounded out the opening notes.

"If ye love me, keep my commandments," sang the choir. Randall stopped them dead at the end of the first line.

"*Someone* in the soprano section is as flat as the proverbial pancake. If you cannot hit the notes, then please don't sing."

Rebecca lightly poked Francesca in the ribs. "Guess who?"

They went through the piece again. Patricia, Francesca noted, continued braying flat notes at top volume. Randall cast Patricia a dark look, but she apparently didn't notice, since her eyes were glued to the music. Mass began promptly at 10 with the choir singing the opening hymn. When it was time for them to sing the psalm with men and women taking turns on the verses, one of the basses, new to the choir, accidentally sang with the women. His mistake prompted a look of unadulterated rage on Randall's face. The man was elbowed quickly by the men near him and silenced.

After he read the Gospel, Father William Snortland carefully adjusted the microphone, causing it to emit a string of embarrassing sounds that sent two teen-agers in the back of the church into a fit of hysterics. The main gist of his sermon was about keeping Advent holy. He mentioned the wheel of the liturgical year. He said that Advent and Lent were both times of preparation and penance. The wheel brought to Francesca's mind the image of a hamster wheel with a little furry creature running on it. *Ignatius,* she thought, *isn't that the name of Father's hamster?* She tried to keep her mind on the thread of his sermon, but she couldn't get the image of the hamster out of her head.

Father William also mentioned a few words about the rules related to genuflecting. Many of St. Rita's parishioners, he said, were growing lax in following the Church's dictates. Francesca remembered that last week he'd talked about the importance of dressing properly in church. Still, as she surveyed the congregation this morning, she noticed that many people were wearing blue jeans and sweatshirts.

Fifteen minutes later, as Francesca tried to stem her tide of yawns, Father William ended his remarks. Next came the offertory prayers and the hymn, and then, before long, the congregation headed to the altar for Communion. After she had received Communion and completed her prayers, Francesca sat studying the line of parishioners waiting to receive the consecrated Host from the priest. She loved to see the way their expressions softened afterwards.

When the choir stood up to sing the anthem, Francesca silently said a prayer that it would go well. She knew from past experience that her own actions could help prayers come true, so she decided to sing very softly and let Rebecca take the lead.

"If ye love me, keep my commandments," the choir sang, "and I will pray the Father, and he will send you another comforter."

Patricia seemed to be going out of her way to pronounce each "r" in spades, but at least she was hitting the notes. And then it happened. Just as the song was drawing to a climax, with the sopranos' voices soaring delicately skyward with the words "That he may bide with you forever," the organ emitted an unexpected, very loud noise. It sounded like a cross between a groan and a moo. In the ensuing shock, many of the choir members lost their places in the music. And although it seemed like an eternity, it was only two seconds before Randall leapt from behind the organ and directed the rest of the piece *a cappella.*

When it was over, Rebecca whispered to Francesca, "Well, we butchered that one, didn't we?"

Randall wasn't looking at the choir, Francesca noticed. *That's a bad sign,* she thought. On the days when it went well, he lavished praise on them. But when there were mistakes, he usually grew silent and moody. *Maybe I don't want to get involved with a temperamental musician,* Francesca reflected. *I think I'd rather have someone more stable.* But at that moment, Patricia rushed up to Randall and gave him a hug, and Francesca felt a surprisingly strong wave of jealously wash over her.

"You were wonderful, but what happened to the organ?" Patricia queried in a loud voice.

With what appeared to be a Herculean act of will, Randall replied quietly through clenched teeth, "I have no idea."

When Mass was over, as Francesca started gathering up her music, she glanced toward the back door, where she saw Father William being accosted by an angry parishioner.

"Let me get this straight, Father," the man growled. "If

I genuflect wrong, that's a sin. If I don't dress right, that's a sin. It looks like the church is filled with potential land mines. Wouldn't it be safer for my soul if I just stayed home?"

Just then, Francesca saw a little girl -- who looked about four years old -- running over to Father William, giggling. The child was carrying a wrinkled piece of construction paper on which there were pasted ragged cotton balls.

"I made this for you," she said.

"It's wonderful!" Father William exclaimed. He accepted the gift and held it as if it were a sacred manuscript from the early centuries of Christianity. Then he turned his attention back to the parishioner.

"I certainly didn't mean to imply that, well, that not genuflecting and dressing too casual were sins. What I meant to say was that…"

But at that minute, the child interrupted him, tugging at his arm and pointing at the paper.

"Those are LAMBS, Father, like the ones Jesus loves!"

Both men looked at each other and then at the child, and Francesca saw them smile.

"The lambs are wonderful! Thank you!" Father William said, reaching down to pat the child on her head.

Then he extended his hand to the man, who was staring a bit sheepishly at the floor.

"I'm very glad you're here at Mass, and I hope to see you next week."

"You got it, Father. No worries. And, er, uh, well, I'm sorry if I was a little steamed."

Just then the child's mother swooped down and

retrieved her.

"Come along, now, love," the mother said. "We're going to light a candle for granny."

The child took her mother's hand and they rushed away.

"Well, Father, you have a good week now," the man said.

Father William smiled and nodded. He looked down at the clumps of cotton on the paper.

"You too."

* * *

Father John came rushing down the aisle. *I'm dying for a cigarette,* he thought. *I'll give them up as soon as the stress around here dies down. After all, I'll need my wits about me to handle the barrage of complaints that will probably result from William's performance today.*

"Father John." He heard his voice being called rather urgently by Randall. The priest stopped by the organ.

"Yes, what is it?"

"Father," Randall said in a voice loud enough to startle the parishioners who were still kneeling in the pews, praying. "I warned you about the organ. It's on its last legs. And the terrible noise it made today is just the tip of the iceberg."

Father John, his nerves frayed to the last thread, didn't appreciate the temper tantrum. He leaned closer to Randall and looked him directly in the eyes.

"As I told you the other night," he said slowly and distinctly, "We can't buy a new one now. So either accept the situation or figure out a way to raise the money." And then he said something he regretted ten seconds later. "Or it might be time to find another job."

Chapter 4

Francesca ladled a generous helping of punch into her glass and took a sip. *Good,* she thought, *it's spiked to a razor-sharp edge.* She'd spent a few hours preparing for the choir get-together, starting with a long, coconut-scented soak in a bubble bath, while Tubs rested nearby on the bath mat. Still, she felt apprehensive about the gathering, and figured the punch would relax her.

The choir rehearsal get-together, held each year to prepare for Christmas, followed a fairly predictable format. Thanks to Father William's efforts, the choir had been made well aware that Advent was a time to prepare spiritually for Christmas, rather than to party, so there was a real effort to focus the get-togethers on the music. Everyone studiously avoided using the word "party," but there was a thin line that sometimes was crossed. The evening opened with light appetizers and drinks, then moved on to rehearsal at the piano with more food and drinks to follow. Each year, the event was hosted by a volunteer from the choir who happened to have a piano at home. This year, Molly Flowers was the hostess.

Sipping her punch, Francesca surveyed the room. She glanced surreptitiously at Randall, who was standing in the dining room talking with Thomas White, one of the tenors. They were known to lock horns on musical selections and she had seen them walking to their cars after choir practice, gesturing rather fervently about an apparent disagreement over choral matters she knew little about. *Judging by the color of Randall's face,* she thought, *he's probably been dipping somewhat freely into the punch bowl.*

Patricia, her hair freshly streaked with golden highlights, was wearing a silky blouse and a snug black designer skirt, short enough to show off her well-toned calves. She was engulfed in her own private cloud of expensive cologne, and her fingernails were gleaming with a blood-red polish that precisely matched her lipstick. As she dipped the ladle into the punch bowl, she gave Francesca a frosty little smile.

"I see you've done something different to your hair."

"Yes, a touch of henna."

"Hmmmm," was all Patricia said.

I'm not going to let her bother me. Francesca helped herself to cheese and crackers. She waved at Molly, who was in the kitchen, replenishing a tray of appetizers. When everyone had first arrived, Molly had given a brief tour of the modest two-bedroom house she'd recently bought, happily pointing out the fireplace and polished hardwood floors. Her 18-pound orange tomcat, Otis, was now stalking through the room searching for cheese crumbs on the floor. Everyone gave him a wide berth, since Otis had a reputation for nipping people that annoyed him.

Rebecca, arriving late, appeared to be in a gloomy mood. "Another loser blind date last night," she confided to Francesca. "He turned out to be shorter than me, and he had one thing he wanted to talk about, which was golf."

Francesca gave her a hug. "Don't get discouraged. You know how it goes: 'You win some, you lose some…'

Rebecca chimed in: "Yeah -- and some bore you to death. But, seriously, my biological clock isn't just ticking; it's going into full alarm mode."

"Come on, folks, let's get started," Randall called out, and the choir members gathered near the piano, taking seats in the chairs Molly had arranged there.

"Before we start, I have an announcement to make. Francesca Bibbo has agreed to be my assistant. So you can get in touch with her for things like sheet music, programs, and so forth. And if you are going to miss a rehearsal or a Sunday morning, please let her know."

Rebecca nudged her and whispered, "Let me know if he asks you to work overtime, OK?"

The choir rehearsed for two hours, taking breaks only to replenish their drinks. There was a long list of music they had to practice for the upcoming Christmas Eve Mass. Randall seemed somehow subdued since his run-in with Father John, Francesca noted. Even when Thomas White and Gavin Stewart, the lead tenors, botched one of the easier pieces, he didn't say a word. His mind was apparently elsewhere. Soon they had one piece left to rehearse – and it was then that Patricia dropped the bombshell.

"Randall, when do I get to practice my solo?"

There was an almost deafening silence in the soprano section.

"Patricia has a solo?" Lily Santiago had a look of horror on her pretty face.

Lily Santiago was as tall and shapely as Patricia was, but had gleaming black hair and exotic features that revealed her Hispanic roots. She was a professional singer in Atlanta with a silken voice that received rave reviews in the newspapers. She always wore sophisticated, trendy outfits and had every gleaming black hair in place. Lily had often voiced her strongly negative opinion of Patricia's singing abilities to the other choir members.

Randall, silent, was staring at the piano as if it were an alien life form that he had never seen before.

"Randall," Lily said slowly, "I didn't realize you had already assigned Christmas Eve solos."

"I haven't made any decisions yet."

"Oh, really?" Patricia piped up. "Well I seem to remember you promised *me* a solo."

What happened next made Francesca wonder how much punch Randall had consumed. Something inside him seemed to snap. He slammed his hand down on the top of the piano with such force that the framed pictures on a nearby wall were jolted out of alignment.

"You have about as much talent for singing as pigs have for flying," he snarled.

Everyone in the choir seemed to be struck dumb for ten seconds. Patricia's face turned scarlet. Then Andy Dull, seemingly unaware of the land mine he was treading on, chimed in, "Hey, Patricia's got a great voice. Give Lily and Patricia both solos, why don't you, and then we can all get something to eat?"

Randall had descended back into silence. He was studying the musical score in his hands as if it were a check for a million dollars endorsed to him. Patricia, lips pressed tightly together, stormed out of the room, her high heels grinding tiny holes in Molly's hardwood floors. Francesca couldn't help but notice that Lily had a triumphant little smile on her lips.

"Alright, folks, I think we've done about as much damage as we're going to for now. Let's take a break," Randall said.

* * *

Father John rang the doorbell a few moments later, and Molly Flowers rushed to answer it. As he walked in, he was sure he had a guilty look on his face.

"So glad you could make it, Father."

Ah, yes, she's the one with that wonderful Southern accent. And thank God she's not a hugger, he thought, making his way to the drinks table.

He tried to make an appearance at most of St. Rita's functions, but he'd almost talked himself out of coming tonight. He and Randall hadn't spoken since the blow-up. Father John was furious with the choir director, who he felt had definitely overstepped his bounds, but he also was somewhat ashamed of the way he had handled the recent confrontation with him.

Not only that, but Father John had received a call from a parishioner to let him know about a petition to the archbishop that was circulating at the church. Although he didn't know for sure, he suspected Randall was behind it. *That's all I need,* he thought moodily, fishing for a pack of cigarettes in his pocket. *Next thing I know, I'll be transferred to some hole-in-the-ground church in the Okefenokee Swamp.*

"Do you mind if I smoke?" he asked the hostess.

"Not at all, Father, go ahead." She gave him a big

smile. But, then, as he lit up, he noticed she made a point of throwing open all the windows in the living and dining rooms. *So much for honesty*, he thought.

He inhaled greedily. He had a new bargain with himself: He'd give up smoking once the holidays were over. After all, the stress of the upcoming season, not to mention the potential mess with the archbishop, would be impossible to withstand without a few vices. Speaking of which, he filled a tumbler full of red wine and then began helping himself to a few thick slices of roast beef.

Molly came over and, before he could stop her, she began talking about her job in labor and delivery. *Please, spare me the details*, he prayed silently.

"We just catch most of them, Father. Once the head emerges, it all happens so fast."

He could feel his face flushing, as he immediately began talking about the weather.

Anything to get her off that topic. As he was mentioning the forecast for the next few days, he saw a tall blonde woman emerging from the kitchen and shooting Randall a very dark look.

The woman began chatting with one of the tenors, and Father John stopped in mid-stream with Molly.

"What is it, Father?" Molly asked.

"Oh, er, nothing, I thought I heard something."

He looked over at the blonde woman. *Could she be Lady Chatterly?*

Just then, Molly made an excuse about having to check on the punch bowl, and Andy Dull took her place next to Father John.

"What do you think about that new ordinance, Father,

the one that's going to make it illegal for homeless people to beg for money downtown?"

It was one of Father's John's hot buttons, the way the city tried to shame poor people.

"If Christ were to visit Atlanta today," he told Andy sadly, "He might be thrown in jail for vagrancy."

"I wonder what Christ would think if He came to St. Rita's."

"What do you mean?" Father John hoped Andy wasn't going to launch into criticism about the parish.

But Andy didn't seem to have any ulterior motive. "Well, I think He would see that we're trying to take care of the poor, what with all the collections for the St. Vincent de Paul Society, and the way folks help out at the homeless shelters."

"Oh, yes, definitely, our parish is very concerned about the poor."

Now Andy stared at the floor. "But what about the music?"

Uh, oh, here it comes. Something about how Christ would buy a new organ or something, Father John thought and took a sip of his wine.

"The music is quite dignified and quite traditional, wouldn't you say?"

"Oh, sure, but to keep it that way, I think we need that new organ, Father, with all due respect."

"As the pastor, I have to be a good steward of the money, Andy. And I really believe the organ can be repaired."

Andy had opened his mouth for a rebuttal, when suddenly Molly walked over and interrupted them.

"Father, would you bless the food before we begin*?"*

Father John quickly put down his plate. "Oh, yes, of course, certainly." *Saved by the belle,* he thought.

* * *

After everyone had eaten their fill, some of the tipsier choir members gathered at the piano and began singing Christmas carols.

"Don't we know any Advent songs?" Molly asked.

"I'm dreaming of an Advent wreath." Andy wrapped a hairy arm around her shoulder.

"Excuse me, I need to get another drink." Molly quickly disengaged herself.

Andy was not one to be discouraged easily. "Rudolph had an Advent Candle, and he lit it every night," he bellowed, "and if you ever saw it, you would say it sure was bright."

There were collective groans from the group gathered at the piano.

"Alright, maybe I'm not a songwriter after all."

Francesca, meanwhile, was keeping an eye on Randall. She noticed that, after a brief hello, he had managed to avoid Father John for most of the evening. But now she saw Randall follow Patricia out onto the back deck. She scooted close enough to the door to peek outside and overhear their conversation. She knew in her heart that what she was doing was wrong, but the impulse to eavesdrop was stronger than her impulse to heed her conscience.

Patricia appeared to be studying the night sky as if the

stars were Tarot cards revealing her future. Francesca saw Randall come up behind Patricia and put his arms around her slender waist.

"Hey, beautiful, are you going to forgive me?"

Patricia turned around to face him.

"Why did you say those horrible things about my singing?"

"Darling, look, you have a lovely voice, you know it and I know it, but how was I going to deal with Lily? I don't want to be *forced* into giving anyone a solo. You were wrong to mention the solo before I had a chance to announce it to the whole group."

Patricia's expression changed. The dark angry look softened – and Francesca felt a true wave of compassion for her. *She really wants to believe whatever he tells her,* she realized.

"Oh, I didn't think of that. But you didn't mean what you said about my singing, did you?"

"Of course not! Your voice is beautiful." Then Francesca saw him draw Patricia near and give her a long, lingering kiss on the lips.

She had seen enough. She felt a quick stab of remorse and guilt as she moved away from the window. Then she headed into the kitchen to pour another glass of wine, nearly colliding with Thomas White. He laughed and gave her a very sensuous blue-eyed look.

He's not very tall, but that's OK, Francesca thought.

"Where are you headed in such a hurry, Mrs. Bibbo?"

"Uh, I was going outside for some fresh air, but I think it's starting to rain."

He looked her over appraisingly from head to toe.

"You sure look pretty tonight. Did you do something different to your hair?"

"Just some highlights." She was pleased that he'd noticed. "Thanks."

A moment later, a slightly disheveled-looking Randall and Patricia walked back into the house. When he saw them, Thomas called out, "Hope there isn't a storm on the way." They looked at him quizzically.

When Father John ambled over to ask Thomas about his graduate studies, Francesca excused herself and headed to the bathroom to touch up her makeup. To get there, she had to go through the master bedroom. As she reached out to open the bathroom door, she felt someone grab her from behind.

"Oh, my gosh!" she exclaimed, and then realized who it was. "What are you doing?" she cried out as Randall embraced her. Then she started to laugh. *I've had too much to drink.*

"Waiting for you, of course." He switched off the light.

He pulled her against him so tightly, she was sure he could feel her heart trying to jump out of her chest. He kissed her, a long, hungry kiss, and she felt her willpower dissolving. She leaned against him, letting out a little sigh like someone devouring chocolate ice cream after a long diet. *Girl, get a grip*, she warned herself.

"I really want to be with you again soon." And then he lightly stroked her earlobe, as if he knew it happened to be one of her most intense erogenous zones. "Alone."

At that moment, the lights flickered on and there stood Lily in the doorway.

"Well, excuse *me*," she said in a tone of voice that could have instantly turned water into ice. "I had no idea this room was occupied. Don't let me disturb you two...love birds."

Randall drew back from Francesca as if he had just learned she had a contagious disease. He straightened the front of his shirt and looked guilty. "I think I've had way too much to drink…"

Lily smiled in a way that mystified Francesca and then exited the room.

Well, thanks a lot, Francesca thought, angered by the implication that alcohol had motivated his kiss, rather than affection.

He must have noticed her expression. "Look, don't misunderstand me. I just don't want to …well, I want to be a gentleman with you, that's all."

She wanted to believe him. "It's alright. Let's just forget it."

He took her hand. "I don't want to forget it, Francesca. Look, I'm no saint. I'm going to level with you. I was outside with Patricia earlier, and I kissed her. Not because I'm attracted to her, but because I was trying to make amends for what I said about her singing earlier. That was wrong, and I know it. But you're special to me. You really are."

She remained silent. She didn't know what to say. *I hope he means it.*

Now he smiled at her. *Those dimples again.* "Are you angry with me? Are you going to quit your job as choir assistant?"

"Of course not." *Let's change the topic,* she thought.

Talk about something safe like work. "But you really haven't given me much work to do so far."

He straightened his tie. "You're right, but I do have a big assignment for you. If you'll go in my office, you'll find all kinds of papers in the desk drawers. Everything is terribly disorganized. Old programs, invoices, you name it. I'm famous for throwing stuff in drawers and forgetting about it. You can take everything home with you, and organize it there."

He took her hand gently. "Would you be interested in putting some order in my life?"

How can I say no? Here's a man who needs me. Isn't that what I miss so much about Dean?

"Yes, of course, Randall, I'll be happy to."

Now he hugged her, but the feeling wasn't romantic. There was almost desperation in the embrace. When he drew back, there seemed to be moisture glistening in his eyes.

"Francesca, some day I want to tell you more about my life. I haven't been…exactly an angel…but I've been trying to change."

"Don't worry about it, Randall. We all have stuff we wish we hadn't done."

"You're the best, Francesca. You're really a godsend. And I think we're going to make quite a team."

It was midnight when the party started breaking up. Francesca had stopped drinking at 10 because she knew she'd be driving home. As people were straggling out into the night, Molly whispered, "Randall looks soused. Maybe you could drive him home?"

"Sure, let me get my purse." But by the time Francesca

returned, Randall had already slipped out. They saw his car pulling out of the driveway.

When Francesca left the party about a half hour later, something told her to drive by his house to check up on him. She knew from the choir list that his house was about a mile away from Molly's. It was one of the refurbished 1940s cottages that were becoming very popular in Decatur. As she slowed down, she could see that the lights in his house were off and his car was parked in the driveway. *All is well,* she thought, and then she felt a distinct temptation to ring the doorbell. *Why not? Would that be so wrong?*

Then she noticed another car out front. A sparkling white Mercedes -- Patricia's. *It looks like Romeo has found his Juliet. Why was I stupid enough to believe anything he said*? She drove home, scrubbed off all her make-up, and put on her pajamas. Then she climbed into bed with Tubs.

"It's you and me, boy, and it's a good thing you're not a human being. Some of us just can't be trusted."

* * *

The next morning, she awakened at eight and had to rush around getting dressed to get to the rectory by nine. Tubs watched her as she dressed, as if fearful she might forget to feed him. But just before she scurried out the door, she up-ended an entire can of tuna into his bowl.

The phone was already ringing as she took her seat at the little desk in the foyer of the rectory. The priests lived upstairs, while the downstairs area contained the kitchen, plus a few offices. "What time are the Sunday masses?" the caller wanted to know. Then a new mother called to sign up for baptism classes, and an unidentified parishioner called to register his complaint about how chilly the church had been last Sunday. "Isn't anyone paying the heating bills?"

When the first wave of phone calls subsided, Francesca wandered down the hall and stopped in Margaret Hennessy's office. Margaret, the director of education, wasn't coming in today, but her office door was open. There was the usual big glass jar of candies on her desk. Margaret was pencil thin and didn't indulge in candy, but she kept the jar full for others. *A nice ministry,* Francesca reflected.

Mmmmmm, Milky Way bars. She put a few in her jeans pocket and started heading back to her desk, but then she decided to stop by Randall's office.

I'm going to forget all about last night and all the romantic stuff he said to me. I'm going to be his assistant and nothing more. I'm not going to act like a jealous idiot just because he has a thing for Patricia.

She unlocked the door and went in. She remembered his description of how disorganized he was. *He wasn't kidding.* There were stacks of papers and music books on his desk, plus old church bulletins, old programs from past Christmases, pencils and pens strewn every which way, and sticky notes with dates and times scribbled on them posted on the desk top. On the sunny windowsill a single African violet plant had birthed a tiny white flower. *I'll bet Margaret Hennessy waters it.*

It was difficult opening the desk drawers because they

were stuffed to capacity. She decided to take everything out and start from scratch in organizing things. She found a very large, empty cardboard box in the corner of the office and upended folders, papers, and musical scores into it. She put the box on the floor and pushed it down the hall, since it was too large to carry. *I'll take it home with me and bring everything back in a few days.*

Just then, the phone began ringing.

"Francesca, it's me, Patricia," a voice on the other end wailed. But it didn't sound like Patricia at all.

"Oh, it's too horrible, I just can't, I can't take it..."

Another line started ringing. "Hold on, Patricia, I have another call. I'll be right back. St. Rita's," she said to the other caller. "Please hold."

"No, ma'am, I won't hold. This is Jack Davis, and I've been a member of the church now for 20 years. But I have to say I've never before heard a sermon about the rules about genuflecting and I just don't understand why we have to be subjected to..."

She did something that she had never done before. She hung up on him, promising herself that if he called back, she'd explain there had been an emergency.

"Patricia? Are you still there? What's wrong?"

"Oh, it's just horrible. I went by Randall's house this morning and rang his bell, but he didn't come to the door. His car was outside, so I was worried something might be wrong. He was awfully drunk last night, you know."

"Well, I went around to the back door and it was open, so I went in." Patricia started sobbing again. "I don't know how to say this," she wailed. "But Randall's dead."

Dead! A wave of nausea swept through Francesca as

she felt herself reliving some of the shock she'd experienced two years ago when she'd learned about Dean's death over the phone.

"Oh, dear Lord! What happened?"

"I don't know. He was on the couch. I thought he was sleeping, but when I tried to get him to wake up, he didn't. And he was, oh, God, he was so cold." She broke down again.

"Patricia, where are you now?"

"I got so frightened that I left and came home."

"You have to call the police. Dial 911 and report his death. Do you understand?"

"Yes, OK, I will," Patricia sobbed, and then hung up.

"AAAGGH!" Francesca dropped the phone. Something hot and fuzzy was slobbering all over her feet. She jumped from the chair and looked downward, her heart beating so fast she thought she was having a coronary.

"Oh, Lord, have mercy! Spot!"

The big mutt beamed at her, his tongue dangling from his mouth.

* * *

A short while later, Father John made his way slowly down the stairs. He had a vicious headache, the result of downing too many glasses of wine last night. He nearly tripped over Spot, stretched out on the kitchen floor, gnawing on a shoe. The priest poured himself a glass of water, then lit a cigarette and took a long, blissful drag. Then he saw Francesca entering the kitchen, looking much worse than he felt.

"What is wrong, my dear?"

"Oh, Father, something terrible has happened. Patricia Noble went to Randall's house this morning and found him." Her voice faltered. "Found him dead."

Father John could feel the blood draining from his face. He stubbed out the cigarette and sat down, while also pulling out a chair for Francesca.

"Dead? What do you mean? What happened? And, here, sit down, you look like you need a chair."

"I don't know what happened, Father. Patricia said she couldn't wake him up."

* * *

A few days later, while Francesca was sorting the mail in Margaret Hennessy's office, the front doorbell to the rectory rang. She heard Father William answering it.

"Police?" she heard him say. "What is this all about?" He had returned from visiting his parents in Valdosta only a few minutes ago, and no one had filled him in on Randall's death.

Francesca quickly returned to her desk in the foyer, where Father William was talking to a rather attractive man. Father John was standing by her desk, fiddling with a pencil.

"I'm Investigator Viscardi with the Decatur Police Department," the man said. "I'm here about Randall Ivy. I'm questioning anyone who might have some knowledge about Mr. Ivy's death."

The officer was olive-complexioned with hair and eyes

the color of espresso. *I'll bet he's Italian,* Francesca thought.

"May God have mercy on his soul!" Father William fished in his pants pocket for his Rosary beads. "What happened?"

"He was found in his home three days ago by a member of St. Rita's choir." The detective's eyes swept over the three people standing before him, resting an extra second on Francesca.

"Were any of you at the choir party?" He reached into his pocket and extracted a pen and small notebook.

"I was," Francesca volunteered. *He has sexy eyes.* Then her conscience elbowed its way into her thoughts. *At a time like this, you're noticing his looks?*

"And you are?" He looked her up and down quickly.

"Francesca Bibbo. I'm in the choir – and I'm… I was… Randall's assistant."

"Miss Bibbo, did you notice anything unusual about Mr. Ivy the night of the party?"

She looked down at the carpet, noting that Spot had chewed a small hole in the edge.

What do I say? That I was falling for him? That I didn't know if I could trust him or not?

"Not really, except that he was drinking quite a bit. When he left the party, it was about midnight, and Molly – she was the hostess – wanted me to drive him home. But he got away too quickly, so I couldn't." For some reason she didn't want to admit that she'd followed him home later.

The detective took some notes. He had strong-looking hands with a nice sprinkling of fur on the fingers. *Quite masculine.*

"You said you were his assistant. What exactly do you do?"

She felt herself blushing for no reason, as she thought about Rebecca's little jokes about overtime. "Mostly help him with clerical stuff, like buying sheet music, keeping track of attendance. And I have a big box of his stuff at home that he wanted me to organize."

This seemed to pique the investigator's interest. "Well, we may want to take a look at his office at some point and maybe the contents of that box. Would you mind giving me your address and phone number?"

I'd love to! Please, God, let him be single!

"Not at all." She wrote the information on an index card and gave it to him.

He smiled in an officious way, but his next question startled her. "Thank you, Miss, or is it *Mrs.* Bibbo?"

"I'm a widow. I still go by Mrs."

Next he turned to Father John, giving him a brief once-over while turning over a new page in the notebook. Father extended his hand.

"I'm Father John Riley, the pastor, and I was also at the party."

"Mr., uh, Father Riley, did you notice anything out of the ordinary about Mr. Ivy that night?"

"We didn't get a chance to speak." Father John tweaked his collar, which had begun chafing him.

"And how would you describe your relationship with him? Did you know Mr. Ivy well?"

"Uh, well, he was the choir director, so of course we spoke frequently, about the musical selections and so on."

Then Father John noticed Father William running his fingers nervously over the Rosary beads, his lips moving in silent prayers. Father John didn't want to let the younger man down.

"There is something else. Randall and I had a disagreement recently. You see, he wanted me, or rather the church, to purchase a new organ. He was very displeased with the one we already have. He had asked me many times. Well, I lost my temper. I told him, more or less, to either accept the situation or, uh, or leave."

"So you threatened to fire him?"

"Well, yes, you could say that. But really he was a fine musician and I wouldn't have..." his voice trailed off.

The officer questioned Father William for a few moments and then left.

* * *

Francesca noticed that the church was filled to capacity for Randall's funeral, since he was well known by most of the parishioners. Margaret Hennessy had arranged for the director from a church downtown to lead the choir in a few traditional funeral pieces. Fortunately, there was the blessed absence of "On Eagle's Wings," which Randall had made fun of at numerous rehearsals ("Every time I hear it, I want to clip the wings on that blasted bird.") Lily Santiago sang a gorgeous solo rendition of "O Divine Redeemer" that had nearly everyone in the church teary-eyed, especially when she sang the words, "Grant me pardon, and remember not my sin." Francesca saw Lily leaving the church in tears when the song was over.

Francesca also learned from Margaret that Randall had no siblings, and his parents were deceased. Still, in the front pew, usually reserved for family members, there was someone who caught Francesca's eye. She looked very young, maybe 20, and she was Lily's height. After Mass, Francesca walked over to the young woman.

"I'm Francesca Bibbo, and I was Randall's choir assistant. I don't think we've met?"

There was a shy smile and the offer of a limp little hand. "No, I haven't been here before. I'm Candy."

"It's so terrible about Randall." Francesca grasped the girl's hand lightly, noting how thin she was. "He was a wonderful musician and the whole choir will miss him dearly."

Candy touched a handkerchief delicately to her eyes. The tip of her nose was red, but it didn't detract from her beauty.

"Yes, Daddy always loved to play music."

Francesca hoped the shock she was feeling wasn't too obvious on her face. "Oh, he was your...your father? I didn't realize. I'm so very sorry for your loss."

"He didn't tell most people about me unless he knew them really well. It's kind of strange, I know. He and my mom got divorced when I was a baby. I grew up with my mom in Miami, so I only saw him about once a year. I moved to Decatur not too long ago, hoping we could get to know each other better, but now..."

"Candy, I have a large box of your father's papers from his office that he wanted me to organize. I haven't had a chance to go through them yet, but it is possible there could be something there you might want. Photos or letters or something like that."

Francesca scribbled her name and phone number on a piece of paper and gave it to the girl. "Why don't you give me a call when you have a chance? Maybe we can get together."

Candy took the paper and tucked it away in a tiny black purse. She sniffed and then smiled. "I would like that."

Chapter 5

Tubs had managed to climb up on a dining room chair. There, he was watching the squirrels scouring the front yard for the bread crumbs Francesca had put out for the birds. Every so often, the old cat would let out a little cry of interest and twitch his tail, as if he were watching a particularly captivating action movie.

Francesca sat across from him in her bathrobe, sipping a cup of coffee and mulling over the story about Randall's death in the morning paper. The paper reported there had been no signs of a struggle or forced entry into his house. The autopsy revealed that Randall had evidently taken an overdose of a prescription drug for insomnia. The death was ruled a suicide, even though no note was found.

As Francesca glanced outside, a single leaf winged its way to the ground like a little yellow bird. It was another snazzy fall day in Decatur with the trees decked out in fanciful colors, and somehow this made the fact of Randall's death seem even more tragic. Something about the police's conclusion bothered her. She didn't doubt the accuracy of the autopsy report, but she had trouble with the notion that Randall had killed himself.

When he kissed me at the party, and when he talked to me, he didn't act like someone who would kill himself a few hours later. Then one of her inner voices chimed in. *People are unpredictable. But why didn't he leave a note?* she countered. *Maybe,* the voice answered, *because he was inebriated. And most drunk people aren't going to get a pen and paper and write a letter.*

She thought about this as she fixed herself a bowl of cereal. *Was it possible that the overdose had been accidental? But Randall was an intelligent man. Surely he would know how dangerous it was to combine pills with booze.*

As she sat lost in thought, she heard Tubs making a peculiar noise. Looking outside, she saw her neighbor's dog depositing a generous pile of manure near her front path. Just as he was lifting his leg to take aim for the birdbath, she put down her spoon and rushed to the front door.

"Go away, Bainbridge! Bad dog!" But the animal, an unkempt German shepherd, simply stared at her. Then she heard her next-door neighbor calling for him.

"Here, Bainbridge, here boy!" The dog scratched at his disheveled ears before deciding to amble home. Myra Findley, her neighbor, had proudly introduced her to the dog a few months ago.

"We don't need a security system at our house," Myra had bragged, as the dog peered at Francesca through yellowish eyes. Bainbridge, it turned out, was a trained attack dog. And Myra was so proud of this fact that she had shared with Francesca the secret words and gesture that would supposedly trigger an attack response in the dog.

"But he's as gentle as a lamb around the kids," Myra had gushed.

Good thing, Francesca had thought, *because Myra has five little kids.* Despite Myra's assurances, it had made

Francesca nervous knowing the dog was wandering around loose in the neighborhood.

What if one day he snaps and lunges for me while I'm out filling the bird feeder? But she had made a real effort to befriend the dog, hoping to win him over. Dog biscuits and an occasional rawhide bone were the offerings she left Bainbridge on her front porch. The result, she now realized, was that the dog felt so comfortable around her, he considered her front yard part of his territory.

Glancing back at the newspaper, she suddenly remembered the box that she had stashed in her back study. *It's time to organize the stuff. Even if Randall doesn't need it anymore, there could be things in there that the church needs, like invoices and old receipts. And there could be photos that his daughter would want.*

She poured another cup of coffee and headed into her study to begin the task. As she upended the box onto the floor, she realized that Randall must have been a true pack rat. There were old phone messages, restaurant receipts, and even envelopes from bills that apparently had been paid. She sighed as she realized how large a task this would be.

First things first. I'll put anything personal in one pile and church stuff in the other. Church bills in one pile, and programs in another. And stuff that is clearly trash in another. As she sorted through the materials, she found a small notebook marked simply "R's recipes." She smiled as she placed it in the personal pile. *I didn't even know he liked to cook.*

And then she unearthed something that really surprised her. Tucked away among church bulletins and handwritten lists of musical selections was a stack of letters bound with a loop of string.

I wonder if these might be letters from Candy.

She untied the string and began to read the first few letters. They were written in black ink in a very elaborate, somewhat old-fashioned handwriting with plenty of flourishes. None were signed, nor were they dated. And someone, she deduced, after reading for a few minutes, certainly had been enamored of Randall.

"I've never known greater joy than when we are together," the author wrote. "My Darling, you make me feel cherished, reborn, and so special." There followed some detailed, almost X-rated descriptions involving the words "ecstasy" and "faint."

This was evidently quite a lurid twosome. But when she glanced over one of the more recent letters, it sounded like the poor woman was despairing of the relationship.

"I'm ready to give up everyone else for you and live with you, but you have to be ready to make a commitment to me as well. I can't wait for you forever, as much as I love you."

I wonder who wrote these. Could it be Patricia? Somehow, I can't imagine her baring her heart like this, but I don't know her that well. And, dear Lord, what do I do now? Do I give these to the police or not? Obviously Randall didn't know these letters were in his desk. He must have wanted to keep them a secret. But if I don't give them to the police, is that withholding evidence? And what about Candy? Would he have wanted her to see these or not? Oh, what do I do?

The phone rang. "Hi, Mrs. Bibbo, how are you?" The

voice on the other end was very young and tentative.

"This is Candy Ivy, Randall's daughter. From the funeral, remember?"

"Oh, yes, of course! How are you doing?" As she spoke, she found herself stashing the letters between some books on her shelves. *I'll figure out what to do about them later.*

There was a sniff on the other end of the line. "I guess I'm OK. I wondered if you'd like to drop by for a cup of coffee. I'm staying at my dad's place."

"I'd love to come by. When's a good time?"

"Any time this morning. I'm just hanging out."

"And the address is?" Francesca asked in a tone that she hoped sounded genuine. Somehow she didn't want Candy to know she already knew where Randall lived.

After hanging up the phone, Francesca dressed in black jeans, a white cotton sweater, and a new pair of suede boots. As she was heading to her car, she forgot about Bainbridge's earlier visit and managed to step smack dab into the fresh pile of dog poop. Her new boots were ruined. Furious, she went back inside and changed her shoes, making a mental note to complain to Myra about the dog's behavior.

* * *

Francesca felt strangely nervous as she pulled into the driveway behind Randall's car. Somehow she expected him to throw open the front door and greet her. He would hug her and then assure her that his death had all been a big joke. But it was Candy who opened the door. She was wearing a pair of skin-tight faded jeans with rips in the knees, plus a sweatshirt with a slogan that proclaimed, “Use me, re-use me, and throw me out.” Francesca was relieved to discover there were some pointers about recycling in the fine print.

“It feels a little weird being here, if you know what I mean,” Candy confided. With her hair pulled back in a pony tail and no make-up on, she looked about twelve years old.

“Don’t sit on the couch, OK? That’s where, that’s where he…where they found him – and I plan to get rid of it as soon as possible.”

“So you’re planning to stay in Decatur?” Francesca settled into a plush armchair.

“Yeah, I think I will. It’s a pretty happening town. Close to Atlanta with all those clubs and malls.”

I hope she’s not one of the many people who worship at a mall instead of a church. Francesca had read somewhere that more people visited malls than churches these days, and Atlanta was becoming the Vatican of consumerism.

“Would you like some coffee and donuts?” Candy asked.

“That’d be nice.”

When Candy got up and went into the kitchen, Francesca felt her eyes drawn morbidly to the couch. She heard Candy rummaging around, making the occasional crashing sound as she evidently located mugs and spoons.

“I hope you don’t mind instant. I’m not much of a cook.” Candy entered the room carrying two mugs.

Francesca suppressed a smile. She had never thought

of freshly brewed coffee as a culinary specialty.

"Instant is fine."

Candy went back into the kitchen and returned shortly with a box of Dunkin' Donuts. As she plopped the box down on the coffee table, Francesca's couldn't help but notice that she seemed like a little girl playing house.

"My big weakness." Candy picked up a chocolate-covered pastry. "I hate Krispy Kremes, though. They're like eating lard."

"I never turn down donuts, no matter what the brand." Francesca was delighted to see a shy smile on Candy's face. *The poor girl needs some cheering up.*

Francesca reached into the box and extracted a donut heavily dusted with cinnamon. "You know, I read somewhere that donuts have some kind of fat in them that is supposed to cause cancer." She took a big bite. "But I don't worry about things like that anymore. Not since doctors reported that dark chocolate and red wine are good for us."

Candy giggled. She had quickly polished off her first donut and was working on her second.

"So what are your plans for the future?" Francesca settled back in the chair.

With her mouth still full, Candy replied, "You know, at first I thought I'd go to beauty school in Atlanta. I've always wanted to do hair, but now I'm not sure. Dad didn't leave me that much money really, but it's enough so I can probably just hang out for a few months and do absolutely nothing."

"Do you think you'd enjoy that?" Francesca was mentally trying to talk herself out of a second donut.

Candy looked startled. Evidently it had never crossed her mind that anyone might doubt that doing nothing would be the epitome of a happy life.

"Oh, you know, I don't mean *nothing*. I'd go to the mall and the movies. And there's always TV."

Francesca didn't reply. If Candy's dream of a good life wasn't a scathing indictment of the younger generation, she didn't know what was. *Oh, quit being so judgmental,* one of her voices chided her. *When you were in your twenties, wasn't your idea of happiness bumming around on the beach and smoking an occasional joint? Guilty as charged,* she admitted.

"It must have been difficult growing up without your father," she said, changing the subject.

Candy poked idly around in the box and extracted a third donut. "Oh, not really. You see, he and my mom didn't get along. They divorced before I really knew him that well."

Candy dabbed at her chocolate-stained lips with a napkin.

"He's – he was – a very talented musician, you know, and mom told me how important his career was to him." There was a loud sniff. "Sometimes family can just get in the way, you know. My mom always told me how proud I should be to have such a great father."

"Yes, he certainly was talented." Francesca now decided to put an end to her mental debate over whether or not to allow herself a second donut. *It's probably psychologically harmful to always be denying oneself.* She reached into the box.

"There were times I wished they'd stayed together."

Candy licked a bit of chocolate from her fingers. "But my mom said it was for the best. Mom used to get so mad at him when they were married. I think they just had very different personalities. She told me once she was mad enough to kill him."

That's an interesting tidbit of information, Francesca mused. *I wonder if Candy's mom was angry at Randall for two-timing her.*

"And where is your mother now?"

Candy studied a small tattoo of a frog on her left arm as if noticing it for the first time.

"My mom? Oh, she lives in Decatur too."

Suddenly the girl's expression changed. She let out another loud sniff, and her lips trembled a bit. She looked so sad that Francesca felt a surge of maternal tenderness sweep over her.

"I always hoped they'd get back together, my mom and dad, but now..." A dark mascara-stained tear trickled down her cheek.

"Oh, excuse me, please." She grabbed a paper napkin and swiped at her eyes. "It's just that all this is so hard to get used to."

"You don't have to apologize, Candy. I know how difficult this must be for you."

Something about all this just doesn't add up, Francesca thought, as Candy continued to sniff and dab at her eyes. *I hate to pry, but how else can I find out what I need to know?*

"Candy, did your dad seem depressed when you last spoke with him?"

"Huh?" Candy seemed startled by the question. "Dad,

depressed? No, not really. He was always a little moody, you know, but I think he was getting better. He told me when I talked to him on the phone the day that he...that he died...that things were looking up for him."

"Was he specific?"

"He said he had an idea about how to get a new organ for the church. He also said something about finally ending a friendship that had been bothering him. And there was some new relationship, I think, someone he thought a lot of…"

Francesca avoided Candy's eyes. *Could that have been me?*

She drank the last bit of coffee and put the mug down on the table. She tried to act as nonchalant as possible. "Any names?"

Candy pulled another donut from the box, tore it into little pieces, and began rolling the dough between her fingers as if it were clay. "No, he never really confided in me that much. But he knew a lot of people."

Yes, and it seems that one of them penned those fiery letters. I wonder if that was the "friendship" he was trying to end.

Suddenly Candy jumped up from her chair. The donut crumbs hit the floor.

"Oh, gosh, look at the time! I'm supposed to get my hair done at Lenox Square in 20 minutes."

Now the girl looked at Francesca as if seeing her for the first time. "Oh, I forgot to ask you about the box of stuff from my dad's office!"

Francesca took a deep breath. "Oh, yes, the box…I've just started going through it."

"Anything in there I might want to have?" Candy asked. "I don't have many photos of him…"

"Uh, I think it's…it's too early to tell. There was so much in there, you see…."

"Oh, yeah, Dad never threw anything away. Well, you let me know, OK?"

"Yes, I will. And thanks for the coffee and donuts." Once in her car, Francesca uttered a prayer to St. Joseph. *Help me to know what to do about the letters.*

* * *

When Francesca got home, the first thing she noticed was Tubs' absence from his usual spot on the couch. She walked down the hall toward her study and heard the distinct sounds of gnawing, combined with enthusiastic purring. *What trouble is that cat getting himself into?* In the study she found Tubs sitting on top of one of the piles of papers that had been in the box. He was chewing on the book marked "R's recipes."

"Tubs, give me that!" She gently removed the slightly tattered book from the cat's mouth. He continued purring and began batting at a laundry receipt, chasing it around the room.

Curious, Francesca opened the book. It was a handwritten journal of some kind, she realized, and definitely not a collection of recipes. *Do I read it or not? I hate to pry, but if I don't read it, how will I know if it is something I should give to Candy or not?*

An hour later, Francesca was curled up on her living room couch with Tubs nestled in a space between her knees. Randall had started the journal a year ago and had written in it about once a week. A lot of the entries were simply ideas about musical pieces he wanted the choir to play. There were also notes on performances he'd attended with his own critical comments on the singers.

"A real dog but with a stunning voice" he had written about one local opera singer. "Sounded like wolves baying at the moon" read another entry about a choral group performance. And there was one that particularly made her smile: "I kept expecting the choral group to start singing 'We are Many Parts' at any moment."

There were journal entries mentioning some of the people he had dated, but no real details. Two people with the initials of "L" and "P" were becoming real pains. *Must be Lily and Patricia wanting those solos,* Francesca postulated. During the last few months, Randall had written in the journal about an increasing sense of hopelessness and gloom. He evidently had hated the job at the CPA firm, which he described as "soul numbing." He yearned to be a full-time musician but didn't see much chance of that.

He was beginning to dread choir performances because something always seemed to go wrong. There seemed to be something else troubling him, but his references were so mysterious, she couldn't tell what was wrong. Was he addicted to something, or worried about alcoholism? One entry read plaintively: "I'm sinking lower and lower. I've got to stop this and get help."

"Doc has prescribed antidepressants and something for insomnia," Randall had written a few months ago, but a more recent entry said, "The medicine isn't doing much good." After the blow-up over the organ with Father John, he had written: "This can't go on. I'm wasting my life."

So that's it, she thought. *He really was depressed, and evidently he was feeling overwhelmed by his problems. What a shame that he didn't confide in anyone. Maybe he was going to confide in me.* Hot tears stung her eyes.

I'm still not over Dean's death, and now I'm mourning the loss of Randall too. Who knows what might have been?

* * *

The next morning she was back at her desk in St. Rita's rectory. It was an unusually warm fall day with the temperature in the sixties. She loved her mornings at the rectory. They were very peaceful, a nice time to catch up on letter writing when the phones weren't too busy. Her older sister lived in Oklahoma and had three grown children, who had become Francesca's pen pals. Today she began writing to the youngest niece, wondering how much to tell her about Randall's death.

As she picked up her pen to start a letter, the blaring noise of an electrical contraption assailed her ears. *Oh, no, a leaf blower.* She went to the front door and peered out. Sure enough, there was a yardman with a leaf blower strapped to his body, spewing smoke everywhere.

It was one invention she deplored. *No wonder heart disease and obesity are on the rise,* she thought darkly. *A rake provides aerobic exercise, and it doesn't pollute. Especially in a city so near Atlanta, with the air growing filthier by the day, you'd think people would avoid leaf blowers like the plague. And then there are sports utility vehicles-—another blight on humanity. Asthma among kids is increasing because of air pollution, but people still drive around in cars the size of barns.* She suddenly smiled. *There I go again. I'm on my mental soapbox. Didn't Jesus say, "Judge not lest ye be judged?"*

Maybe I should run for political office, she mused. "If elected, I promise to outlaw leaf blowers and SUVs," she envisioned herself proclaiming to the crowds. Then she pictured the crowds hurling rotten fruit at her.

The phone rang. "St. Rita's -- Mrs. Bibbo speaking."

Even though many women of her generation had assumed the title of "Ms.," she enjoyed the more old-fashioned approach. Francesca had been delighted to take Dean's last name upon marriage and to place the lovely title of "Mrs." in front of it. She was actually relieved to be rid of her maiden name, which had been largely unpronounceable: Andriuolo. Some of her feminist friends had been horrified that she had not hyphenated her last name with his, but she had replied: "Francesca Bibbo-Andriuolo? Are you serious?"

The voice on the other end was a very nice one. Rather deep.

"Hello, Mrs. Bibbo, I don't know if you remember me, but this is Tony Viscardi from the Decatur Police Department."

A pleasing image of the handsome officer flashed through her mind. "Yes, I remember. And please call me Francesca."

"Well, Francesca, this isn't a professional call, and I hope it's OK to call you at work."

"Oh, it's not actually work. No pay involved." She glanced down at the pin on her shirt that read: "Don't yell at me. I'm just a volunteer."

"And personal calls are allowed," she added. Her curiosity was definitely piqued. *What could the handsome investigator want that was personal?*

"Well, I won't keep you long. I was wondering if you might like to have dinner with me tomorrow night. We could go to that new Italian restaurant downtown."

That's the same place I went with Randall. Still, if that's where the cute police guy wants to go, I think I can make the sacrifice and eat more Italian food.

"That would be lovely." She began mentally surveying her closet and wondering what she would wear.

"I'll come by at seven. I have your address. You live very close to St. Rita's, I noticed. Do you, by any chance, bike over to the church?"

She cringed. It was one of those promises she kept making to herself. She knew biking would be better for her health and better for the environment than using the car. *I plead laziness*, she thought, *probably just like the guy with the leaf blower.*

"Sometimes, yes." *Well, it's a white lie.* She envisioned her bike in the basement with its two flat tires.

"Be careful. Decatur's roads aren't very biker friendly."

After the phone call, she sat at her desk staring at the calendar while her mind spun out a few fantasies. *He's Italian and he is definitely good-looking. He has an interesting job. Watch out*, another voice said bluntly, *he may be too good to be true. Besides, how do you know he's not married?* The bubble burst.

Just then, Margaret Hennessy stepped into the foyer. "Good morning, dear, it's so nice to see you today. I don't know what we'd do without you."

Francesca beamed. Margaret was one of those people who had a gift for making others feel important. In her early sixties, she was a tall woman who nearly always had a little smile playing on her lips as if she were savoring a private joke. Her brown eyes always had a merry glint. She was listed as the director of education in the church bulletin, but some of the parishioners jokingly referred to her as "Father Margaret" behind her back because she did so much for the congregation.

Now Margaret grew serious. "I was just watering the plant in Randall's office. What a shame. I still can't quite believe he's gone. The last time I spoke with him, he was really looking forward to the Christmas Masses. And he seemed hopeful about raising money for a new organ. I told him I'd do everything in my power to persuade Father John to match any donations Randall was able to get. He really seemed pleased."

"Do you recall when that was?"

"Oh, yes, it was the morning of the choir party, I mean get-together. The same day he committed suicide."

Outside, the leaf blower shut off. The rectory momentarily was bathed in an ocean of silence, at least until someone down the block revved up a chain saw.

"It's hard to tell with some people," Margaret continued. "Sometimes they have their own personal demons that no one knows about. There was probably something quite serious bothering him. I just wish he'd shared it with one of us, so we might have helped him."

"We never know when our time will come, do we?" she added. "I was just reading the New Testament passage about the wise and foolish virgins, and how some weren't ready when the bridegroom arrived."

The words "bridegroom" and "virgin" stirred up a few decidedly romantic images in Francesca's mind. She saw herself and the handsome police officer toasting each other with champagne at their wedding reception. *Oh, where did that come from?* She felt a tide of hot blood rush into her face. *It's been two years since Dean's death, and sometimes the loneliness is just too much. Thank God Margaret can't read minds.*

"A penny for your thoughts," Margaret smiled. "You're awfully quiet today."

Francesca was sure her face was now bright red. "I was just reflecting on the passage you mentioned, that's all. And wondering if I'll be ready when the, uh, bridegroom arrives in the night."

"I'm sure you will be, dear."

Chapter 6

Francesca had never seen this particular waitress before in the Italian restaurant. *She definitely wasn't working the night I was here with Randall.* The girl, who looked about 18, sported a shaved head with her one remaining lock of hair dyed chartreuse. She also wore a silver ring in one nostril, and had an array of colorful tattoos snaking up her bare arms and encircling her neck.

Francesca noticed Tony looking at the girl quizzically. *How will the next generation outdo this one?* she wondered. *Maybe, 20 years from now, kids will be nailing spikes through their heads. Of course, in my youth, I was prancing around in teeny-weeny bikinis and miniskirts and smoking cigarettes, and I turned out fine – I think.*

"What'll ya'll have?" the girl drawled dully.

"Why don't you tell us about your specials?" Tony asked politely.

While the waitress glumly recited the list, Francesca took a sidelong look at Tony. He was every bit as handsome as she had remembered. Her eyes rested briefly on the ring finger of his left hand. His hands were well-tanned, but there was no telltale white mark like you might expect on the finger of a man who'd removed his wedding band for the evening. *But maybe he doesn't wear a ring at all.*

The waitress, yawning widely, took their orders and disappeared into the kitchen. Suddenly, Tony reached across the table and took Francesca's hand. "You look lovely tonight."

When he touched her hand, a shock of surprising energy jolted through her. She wondered if he'd felt it too. *What's happening to me, if even a simple touch is enough to make me melt? It's been a long time since you've had a really romantic evening*, one of her mental voices warned, *so be careful.*

Then he gave her hand a gentle squeeze and her heart began racing. The nagging little voice whispered: *He's handsome, sexy, and he's employed, which means he's too good to be true.*

She wondered if he could feel her pulse pounding in her hand. "Tony, do you have...family in the area? I mean, are you from Decatur originally?"

He gently released her hand. "I was born in Elmhurst, New York, but my parents moved down to Decatur when I was seven. So I guess I'm almost a native."

What lovely eyes he has. And good strong eyebrows. Very masculine.

He paused as the waitress arrived with a bottle of Chianti and two glasses. After a short struggle, the girl managed to uncork the bottle and pour them each a glass. She'd added a large wad of gum to her mouth, giving the impression of a cow chewing its cud, nose ring and all.

After they toasted, Tony continued. "My parents passed away about ten years ago, but I have two sisters in Florida, plus some nieces and nephews." He took a sip of wine.

"I never married. I dated a woman for five years, and I thought we were going to tie the knot, but it just didn't work out. The kind of work I do, the whole homicide thing, well, it's hard on relationships. It's not the kind of job you leave at the office." He sighed. "The worst part is that if you're not careful, you can lose faith in humanity."

So he really is unattached. She was tempted to pinch herself to be sure she wasn't dreaming, given the dearth of available heterosexual males in the metro-Atlanta area. She hoped she didn't look too ecstatic.

"But enough about me," he said. "Tell me something about yourself."

"Well, I'm a Miami girl at heart. That's where I grew up, and I had hoped to live there after college – I went to the University of Florida – but, well, my husband's job brought us to Georgia."

"College, huh? Now I'm impressed. After high school, I went straight into the police academy and then started working. But I always wanted to get a degree. So what did you major in?"

"Philosophy -- something totally impractical, but it fascinated me at the time."

Just then, she glanced across the restaurant and saw two familiar figures huddled together in one of the booths. *That looks like Candy. And the other woman is definitely Lily. I wonder what they're doing here together.*

He refilled their glasses. "What made you choose that major?"

"I think I was searching for something -- life's bigger meaning. It's strange because in a way I already had many answers from childhood. You see, I was raised Catholic but sort of got off track in college."

"Well, we have that in common," he said. "I went to

Catholic schools from day one all the way through high school, but…" His voice trailed off and he fidgeted with his glass.

"Something happened?" she asked.

"Well, it's nothing too original. At some point, I just stopped going to Mass, much to my mother's horror. But I still think of myself as Catholic, and, well, who knows? I might start going again one of these days."

She didn't say anything, but she felt a deep sense of relief that he wasn't a diehard atheist. *Maybe he'll start going to church with me.*

"Did you ever find it?" Tony asked as the waitress brought their salads.

"Find what?"

"Life's meaning."

She laughed. "Yes, I'm pretty sure I did, but it wasn't in any of my college books."

As they began eating their salads, she found her eyes returning now and again to the two women, who were deeply engrossed in conversation and apparently unaware of her. When the waitress brought the entrees, Francesca brought up Randall's death.

"I read in the paper that he'd taken an overdose, but I found myself wondering what he washed it down with."

Tony took a roll from the basket and buttered it, as if he were stalling for time. Was it her imagination or did he look uncomfortable? *Maybe he's not supposed to discuss the case.*

She went on: "You see, I went out with Randall once, and I was just starting to work as his assistant. I didn't know him extremely well, but something about the whole suicide angle doesn't seem right to me."

Tony smiled. "You did say you majored in philosophy, right, not psychology?"

"True, but I minored in psychology. I guess I took just enough courses to be dangerous. I love to know what makes people tick."

"Well, I suppose there's no harm in my telling you," Tony said. "The details, according to the medical examiner's report, are pretty straightforward. It seems Randall had three generous shots of Scotch and a few cups of coffee too."

The waitress delivered the entrees to the table with a big sigh. "Ya'll need anything else?" Her expression clearly communicated her deepest hope that they would make no further demands on her.

"We're fine," Tony said.

Francesca took a bite of the eggplant parmesan, which was tender and delicious, almost as good as her own mother's recipe. "Why would someone planning to commit suicide make themselves a pot of coffee?" she wondered aloud.

"We don't know the actual sequence of events. He could have made the coffee when he got back from the party. Then he might have had the booze later."

As they ate their meal, Francesca took occasional glances at the two women across the restaurant. They seemed deep in conversation, and she noticed some rather elaborate hand gestures from Lily, who seemed to be driving home an important point to Candy.

The waitress plunked down the check on the table as soon as Tony and Francesca had finished their entrees, and turned to walk away.

"We'd like dessert and coffee," Tony said evenly, and she stomped off, returning in moments with the dessert menu.

As they were getting ready to leave, Francesca noticed that Lily and Candy were still having dessert. Their booth was located directly behind the cashier's station. The two women seemed deeply engrossed in their conversation and apparently did not notice her, so, as Tony paid the check, Francesca managed to catch a few tidbits of the rather loud discussion.

"You've got to find something constructive to do with your time," Lily said.

"What's wrong with shopping and just hanging out?" Candy countered.

"I said 'constructive.' I don't want you wasting your life."

There was a pause. "Mom, tell me something: Why are the things I like to do a waste of time, but anything you do is somehow valuable and… and… constructive?"

That was all Francesca heard before she and Tony exited the restaurant. But her curiosity was now at high ebb. *So Lily is Candy's mom!* She did a quick flashback to the night of the choir get-together. She recalled Lily's reaction to seeing Randall kissing her. *It's starting to make more sense now.*

* * *

Francesca awoke the next day feeling very chipper. Tony had been a complete gentleman, stopping in for an after-dinner drink of Benedictine and brandy at her house. He had scratched thoroughly under Tubs' chin, eliciting a pleased rumbling sound from the old cat. That was it. No attempt to put the moves on her, and it was just as well.

Before she had met Dean, she had made the mistake of jumping into bed with a very attractive man she was very much in love with. She had thought he was serious about her, and she had been extremely devastated the next day when he had acted as if nothing had happened. The next week, he had failed to call her for their usual date. She had been forced to face the obvious fact, which was that she had made a huge blunder.

But the experience had taught her something. After marrying Dean, she had realized that sex without the emotional warmth and commitment of marriage was about as enjoyable as eating a gourmet meal out of Styrofoam containers.

Yawning and rolling over in bed, she was momentarily startled by the fuzzy warmth of Tubs, who had sneaked to the top of the bed during the night. He let out a little warning meow as if to alert her. As she lay in bed, the image of Lily and Candy kept nagging at her.

If Lily is Candy's mom, then why do they seem to be hiding the fact? And if Randall and Lily had once been married, why had they kept their past a secret? Something isn't right here. I'm going to swing by Randall's house and see Candy again. Maybe I'll bring her something from the box of stuff. Not the letters, of course, but some item that she might want as a keepsake.

She riffled through the piles of stuff on her study floor and came up with a perfect item: A few photographs of

Randall with the choir, taken about a year ago. An hour later, she parked in front of Randall's house and rang the doorbell. There was no answer, but the front door was unlocked. She poked her head in and called out, "Anyone home?" No reply.

Then she gently eased open the door and stepped inside. *Candy might be out snaring another box of donuts. Well, I'll wait a few moments for her.*

She went into the kitchen and took a quick look around. Dirty dishes were piled everywhere, along with greasy frying pans on the stove. It looked like Candy was attempting to expand her cooking abilities beyond instant coffee and had used nearly every utensil in the kitchen in the process. There was a dishwasher, but it was also full to the brim.

Francesca noticed the doors to the big pantry in the kitchen were open. The shelves were crowded with assorted spices, plus flour, olive oil, a bag of onions, a few clusters of garlic, along with glass jars filled with cereal, rice, and dried beans. But Randall had also devoted some space in the pantry for a selection of alcoholic beverages. There was a wine rack well-stocked with an assortment of imported wines.

What am I looking for? She stared at the wine rack. Then it hit her: This was apparently where he kept his booze, but there were no bottles of hard liquor at all. No bourbon, rum, vodka – and certainly no Scotch, which was what he had drunk on the night he died.

Was Randall a Scotch drinker? She remembered the evening they'd gone out together. He'd only had wine. And at Molly's party, even though there were bottles of the hard stuff on the drinks table, she'd seen Randall concentrating on the wine.

Then where had the Scotch come from on the night he died? Did someone visit him and carry a bottle of Scotch along? And maybe encourage him to get even drunker than he already was? Did that same someone put the sleeping pills in his drink?

Just then, she heard a car pull up outside. *Candy must be back. Well, I'll just give her the photos and head out.* But when she peered out the window, it wasn't Candy she saw hurrying up the walkway. It was Lily. Her heart beating furiously, Francesca followed her first instinct, which was to hide. She edged her way into the pantry and shut the doors behind her. *I don't think she'll know it's my car, so I'm safe on that score.*

Then she heard Lily push open the front door and call Candy's name. Next she heard the sound of high-heeled footsteps as Lily entered the living room.

What do I say if she opens the pantry? "I just came by to borrow a cup of sugar?"

But Lily didn't come into the kitchen. Instead, she went stomping through the other rooms in the house, and Francesca could hear the sound of drawers opening and shutting. She could also hear the sounds of what had to be muttered Spanish curses as Lily tore through the closets.

I wonder what she's looking for. It sounds like she's really desperate to find something – but what? Is it possible Lily had something to do with Randall's death? Hadn't Candy said her mother had once been angry enough with Randall to kill him?

"Where the hell are those letters?" Lily was evidently

talking aloud in frustration. "I've spent too many years cleaning up after that man! Now he's dead and I'm still picking up the pieces!"

A few moments later, Francesca heard the staccato sound of footsteps clicking their angry way to the front door. Then she heard the door slam. She waited a few seconds and then emerged from the pantry and peered out the window. She saw Lily getting into her car, and then watched as the car pulled out in a furious rush from the driveway.

Francesca quickly exited the house, uttering a silent prayer of gratitude that she hadn't been discovered. Then, as she was getting into her car, she had an idea.

Why don't I see what I can learn from the neighbors? Maybe I can find out if anyone heard Randall arguing with someone the night he died. I'll start with the next door neighbor, but I will need some pretense to knock on the door. I know, I'll say I'm thinking of buying a home in the area, and I'm curious about the neighborhood. That should work.

She decided to park her car on the next block, so Candy wouldn't notice it in case she returned. Then she walked back to Randall's street and rang the doorbell on the house next door to his. A heavily wrinkled woman of about seventy answered the door. Her head was wreathed in bright pink foam-rubber curlers, and she was squinting as she took a drag on her cigarette. Francesca gave her a big smile.

"Hello, my name is Francesca Bibbo, and I'm hoping to buy a house about a block away from here. Would it be OK if I ask you a few questions about the neighborhood?"

The woman, who identified herself as Mrs. Gladys Brumble, fingered a roller on her head. Then she inhaled deeply on the cigarette. She looked reluctant.

"Well, I got my soaps starting in a few minutes, but come on in."

Francesca thanked her profusely and took a seat on the couch, which had to be at least a hundred years old, judging from the musty smell and the groaning of the springs. She noticed a cluster of dust bunnies languidly making their way around the room, thanks to a slight breeze from the open window. She reached in her purse and took out a little note pad.

"Do you like living here? Are people friendly?"

"It's OK by me. I have no complaints." Mrs. Brumble sucked on the cigarette as if it were an oxygen line.

Francesca jotted down a few notes and tried to sound as casual as possible with her next question.

"Wasn't there a death recently in the area? I think I read about a suicide in the newspapers?"

Mrs. Brumble brightened considerably. "Yes, it was my next door neighbor, Randall Ivy." She seemed proud of this bit of notoriety.

"Oh, I'm sorry to hear that. Did you know him well?"

Mrs. Brumble took her time inhaling the last dregs of carcinogens from the dying cigarette. Then she stubbed it out in a loaded ashtray that had "See Rock City" printed in red on the side. Next she pulled out another cigarette and lit it up. Francesca tried to edge as far away as possible from the noxious blue stream wafting its way in her direction.

"Not really and it's just as well. You see, he'd

sometimes play this opera music so loud it'd nearly split my skull open. Then one day, Scotty, my grandson – he's 19 and lives with me – was playing some rap music." She paused to cough and flick the ash off the cigarette. "Randall came over here all bent out of shape."

With her hair in rollers and trails of smoke curling out of her nostrils, the old woman momentarily brought to Francesca's mind the image of a dragon in a beauty salon.

"I won't even tell you the terrible things he said to my grandson about rap music," Mrs. Brumble continued passionately. "'To each his own' I always say. Some like Mozart, some like Boyz in the Hood. It's all music, ain't it?"

The old lady nudged a dust bunny with her shoe and looked pleased with her analysis.

Francesca decided to avoid a discussion of music with Mrs. Brumble. She was still trying to digest the image of Randall confronting someone who was playing rap music.

"That night, the night he died," Francesca said, "did you see or hear anything strange?"

"Strange? Well, no, not really. I don't watch my neighbors, you know. I'm not nosey."

She trumpeted another cigarette cough. "But that night I was having trouble sleeping. And I did notice something. It was real late when he came home, and just a few minutes later, another car pulled up in front of the house. A tall blonde lady got out and went into his house."

That had to be Patricia.

"Of course the newspapers said she was a lady friend of his from the choir." Mrs. Brumble's eyes glinted. "But if you ask me, he sure had a lot of lady friends. Just that very night, *another* one came by – about an hour after the first one left."

"Did you recognize her?"

Mrs. Brumble shook her head and a few of the rollers trembled. "No, it was too dark."

"Could she have been the same woman returning for some reason?"

The old lady looked pensive. "Naw, somehow, she looked…I dunno…different. I can't say why for sure, but just…different."

"What about her car?"

"I didn't see no car. She might of parked it down the block."

"How long did the second woman stay?" Francesca hoped her questions wouldn't arouse the old lady's suspicions.

"I don't know. I fell asleep right after that."

Just then, Francesca noticed a rubber tree plant dying from thirst in the corner of the room. Mrs. Brumble saw her glance and said proudly, "That's my grandson's. He likes to garden."

Francesca smiled and shifted on the couch. "Do the police know there was a second woman?"

The old woman nervously fingered her wedding band. "No, I didn't tell them nothing. I don't like no one snooping around, especially the police. It makes me nervous, and my nerves ain't so good."

Now Mrs. Brumble looked anxiously at the TV screen, which dominated the living room like a giant's leering eye. She stood up and looked pointedly in Francesca's direction. “Well, I gotta watch my programs, so...”

Francesca took her cue. She stood up quickly, said her goodbyes, and started toward the door. But before she could leave, a young man clumped heavily into the room. He was wearing scuffed black boots and a leather jacket with various chains dangling from his wrists. There were numerous intricate black tattoos adorning his hands. He was over six feet tall and his head was shaven. His expression was none too friendly.

This must be the Rap Meister, Scotty.

“What’s she doing here?” Scotty gestured toward Francesca.

Mrs. Brumble tweaked one of her rollers. “This lady’s looking to move into a house on the next block. She was asking me questions about the area.”

Scotty cast Francesca a dark look. “Well, I got news for you, lady: There ain’t no house for sale on the next block that I know of. And I don’t like people poking their noses in our business for any reason.”

What a charming lad, Francesca thought, as he started to move toward her, the rank smell of his leather jacket assailing her nostrils. She quickly darted around him and opened the front door.

“I just spoke to a realtor and it seems 211 on the next block will be on the market in a week or so,” she lied brightly and then quickly exited the house. Then, praying that there really was a house numbered 211 on the next block, she hurried to her car.

That afternoon, Francesca made herself a cup of tea, grabbed a couple of butter cookies, and curled up on the couch with Tubs. *If someone had given Randall an overdose of sleeping pills, it was probably someone he knew – or he wouldn't have let them in his house that night. And it was likely that the person was a Scotch drinker who'd brought a bottle along.*

But sleeping pills would be hard to disguise, whether you put them in Scotch or coffee. They would probably float to the top. And even if he were completely plastered, wouldn't Randall have noticed them? She munched thoughtfully on a cookie and took a sip of tea.

And who are the likely suspects? First there's Patricia. But the police knew she had visited Randall that night, and they had already questioned her. What about the second mystery woman Mrs. Brumble claimed she had seen? Could that have been Lily?

She knew that Lily and Randall were divorced, but perhaps Lily had been hoping for reconciliation. And Lily might have been infuriated when she noticed Randall's attention to other women. But there was also Candy, although it was hard to imagine her killing anyone, especially her own father. Still, she would have had a motive too, since she did inherit his house.

Either one of them could have been Randall's second visitor that night.

Francesca poured another cup of tea. *Was there anyone else who might have wanted Randall dead?* She was startled by the image that flashed into her mind: Father John. The two men had argued, and it was rumored that Randall had started circulating a petition to the archbishop.

But Father John wouldn't hurt a fly, protested a voice in her head. *Still, he did have quite a temper,* another one countered. And even if Randall had been visited by two women that night, Father John still could have dropped by later, after the second woman had left, and Mrs. Brumble had fallen asleep.

Another image entered her mind: Mrs. Brumble's grandson, Scotty. *Maybe the argument about rap music was just the tip of the iceberg. With a neighbor like Scotty Brumble, I imagine there'd be plenty of opportunity for conflicts. And maybe that's why Scotty didn't want me asking his grandmother questions because he has a guilty conscience.*

When the phone rang, she jumped nervously, spilling her tea. She wasn't accustomed to thinking about people she knew as potential killers. *Maybe I should just drop this whole thing,* she thought, as she picked up the phone, breaking her usual rule about letting the machine handle her calls.

A gruff male voice, one she didn't recognize, rasped at her: "Listen, you witch, keep your nose out of other people's business, unless you want to end up like the choir boy." Then the person, whoever it was, banged the phone down.

"Oh, my God!" She was shaking, and her knees nearly buckled under her.

The voice had been dripping with venom. She'd never had anyone threaten her like that. Grabbing her telephone book, she looked up the Decatur police department, and then dialed the number, her fingers trembling.

"Decatur Department of Public Safety." It was a real person instead of a recording, Francesca noted gratefully.

Her voice sounded strange to her own ears. "Is Tony

Viscardi there?"

"One moment, please." It seemed like an eternity, but it was just seconds before she heard his voice, which had a magical, instantly calming effect on her.

"Tony Viscardi speaking."

She took a deep breath, and the words rushed out, while tears slid down her cheeks: "Tony, it's Francesca. I'm at home. I just had a very disturbing phone call and..."

"I'll be there in ten minutes."

She sat on the couch and found herself weeping out of sheer nervousness and fear. But there was something else. Tony's immediate impulse to drop everything and come to her rescue reminded her so much of her beloved Dean. He had always been there whenever she needed him. She picked up Tubs and wept into his scruffy neck.

It was less than ten minutes when the doorbell rang. She ran gratefully to the door.

"Tony, thank you so much for coming over. I…I…" And then she broke down and cried.

"Sit down, just relax, and you can tell me everything that happened." He gently led her to the couch.

"Do you have any wine in the kitchen?" She nodded, and he was back in a minute with a glass for her to drink.

"This will help you relax a bit." She accepted it gratefully, remembering childhood when her mother had poured her a glass of milk before bed.

He sat beside her and listened carefully while she related the whole story. Her suspicions about Randall's death. How she'd found out that Lily was Candy's mom. How she'd gone to Candy's house and hid while she heard Lily searching for something. She could tell he was worried.

"I really wish you wouldn't get involved in this, Francesca. There's really no reason for you to be investigating."

"I know…and, Tony…" *I might as well tell him everything.* "There's more. I also visited Randall's neighbor Mrs. Brumble. Her grandson, Scotty, was pretty disturbing." She described his ominous appearance and his rude way of talking.

There was a big sigh. "Francesca, there's no reason to be going around questioning people. This is an open-and-shut case of suicide. Besides, I've already questioned Mrs. Brumble."

She nodded guiltily, taking a sip of the wine. "Something about the case doesn't make sense to me, Tony. I can't explain it, but I have the feeling that someone killed Randall."

"You've been watching too many police stories on TV." He smiled and then leaned over to smooth her hair. When his hand lightly touched her forehead, she had an immediate sense that she was protected and safe. *Maybe he's right. Maybe I'm making a big deal out of nothing.*

Tony helped himself to one of the cookies on the coffee table. "Randall had been drinking at the party. It seems he had more to drink later. Sometimes, when people have too much to drink, they do things on impulse -- stupid, dangerous things. Most of the time, they wake up the next day and regret it. But in Randall's case, what he did was deadly. And the next day never came. It's a real shame, Francesca, but he brought this on himself."

She took another sip of wine. She was starting to relax. "But why was there all the secrecy about Lily?"

Tony brushed a crumb from his jacket. "I knew Lily was Candy's mom."

"You knew?"

"It came out during the investigation. It seems Randall and Lily had an agreement to keep their past quiet. So they just didn't mention the divorce. And Randall wasn't keen on people knowing he had a daughter. Evidently he felt it didn't suit his image, so Candy obediently stayed in the background."

"So much secrecy," she sighed. "It seems like a lot of wasted energy to hide so many things."

"It does to me too, but I've seen it before. People think they can just lay the past to rest by ignoring it. Unfortunately, it nearly always rears its ugly head again."

Tubs climbed into Tony's lap, and Francesca tried to remove him. She knew Tubs had a habit of shedding profusely. But Tony just shrugged. "That's alright. He and I are becoming buddies."

She remembered how Tubs had nipped Randall that day. He seemed to be taking quickly to Tony, however. Then her thoughts returned to the matter at hand.

"But Candy didn't hide the fact that Randall was her father when I met her at the funeral."

Tony nodded. "She probably figured it didn't make any sense to keep the secret going any longer with her father dead."

"Something Mrs. Brumble said is troubling me," Francesca said. "She mentioned seeing a *second* woman visiting Randall's house that night."

Tony raised an eyebrow. “I don’t know what kind of game Mrs. Brumble is playing. When I questioned her, she never mentioned a second woman. But she doesn’t seem like the most reliable witness, Francesca, so she might just have been pulling your leg.”

“That’s possible. But why did I get that horrible phone call? Who could that have been?”

“From what you’ve told me, I’ll bet it was Scotty Brumble. People who have something to hide tend to react like he did when anyone starts asking questions. I don’t know for sure, but from your description of him, it’s certainly possible Scotty is into something illegal, maybe drugs. And I don’t think he bought your story about checking out the neighborhood.”

She thought it over. “It didn’t really sound like him on the phone, but I only met him once, and…well, I guess he could have been disguising his voice, right?”

He smiled. “That’s right.” He put his arms around her. “Listen, Francesca, you know what I advise?”

“What?”

“I think you should stop analyzing everything. You should stop playing psychologist.”

He drew her nearer. She could feel his clean-shaven cheek against her own face. *How lovely.* She could hear his nice even breath in her ear and feel his heart racing beneath his crisp white shirt.

“You’re very sweet.” He gave her a light kiss on the lips, as he held her so lovingly. He stroked her hair. “Such soft hair.” Then he straightened up. “And you’re a very tempting lady. But I have to go, darling. I have to get back to work.”

"But promise me one thing." He stood up. *Anything,* she thought, *anything, just call me "darling" again.*

"Sure, what is it?"

"Leave the police work to me. And if you get any more phone calls or any trouble of any kind, call me right away."

It was then that she very sheepishly told him about the journal and love letters. She felt like she sometimes did in the confessional, painfully shy while telling her sins to the priest, then immensely relieved once she received absolution. She then unearthed the journal and love letters and handed them over to him.

"I didn't know what to do with these, whether they should go to Candy or not," she said. "But I think they would do more good if you had them. Maybe they'll give you more insight into the case."

He riffled through the journal quickly. Then he looked at the first letter. "Do you know who wrote these?"

"I have no idea. None of them are signed. But after you've read them, you'll see that it was someone Randall was definitely involved with romantically."

"Alright, Francesca, now is there anything else you want to tell me?"

I think you're handsome. And extremely kind.

"No, that's it. I swear I've 'come clean,' as they say in the cop movies."

He laughed. "OK, now, you take it easy the rest of the day. I'm going to do some investigating on that phone call. I'll let you know as soon as I find something out."

I should prepare supper and feed Tubs, she thought after Tony left. But she just lay on the couch for a while.

She luxuriated in the memory of the handsome investigator's kiss until Tubs wandered into the kitchen and meowed plaintively.

Chapter 7

Father John was pacing nervously in his room. Ever since Randall's death, he'd been having trouble sleeping. An hour ago he'd awakened from a dream in which the choir director had stormed down the aisle during his sermon and screamed at him: "Hypocrite, hypocrite!" The entire congregation had stood up and applauded. Then Randall suddenly had been transformed into Little Richard, and the congregation had started stomping their feet and waving their hands, singing in unison, "I'm Gonna Cross the River Jordan with Jesus in My Heart."

That's when Father John had realized he was dreaming, because there was no getting around it: His congregation didn't sing. And forget the clapping and stomping; they just weren't into that at all. Then, to his horror, the dream had taken a sharp turn, and he'd found himself in the confessional. The woman behind the privacy screen suddenly pushed it over and plopped down on his lap. He couldn't clearly see her face, but he knew who it was: Lady Chatterly.

"Bless me, Father, and then let's sin," she whispered. But seconds later, the confessional door opened and there stood Father William in his pajamas. He was carrying a cage with his pet hamster running maniacally on its wheel. At that point, the dream vixen had gone running from the confessional. She had paused only to deliver a disturbing line to the two men: "I know who killed him."

He'd awakened with a start, overcome with anxiety. He had immediately rummaged for his rosary beads in the bedside table. As he paced, he began reciting a steady stream of Hail Marys to calm himself. As always, the words nudged the train of ugly and disturbing images off his mental track, slowly giving him a sense of peace. He meditated on the sorrowful mysteries of the rosary: the agony in the garden, the scourging of Jesus, the crowning with thorns, the carrying of the cross, and the Crucifixion.

After the Rosary, he lit a cigarette and glanced at the clock. It was 3 a.m., and three o'clock, whether it was a.m. or p.m., was considered a mystical time. It was the hour that St. John of the Cross had called the "dark night of the soul," because, according to tradition, Christ had died on the cross at 3 p.m.

From down the hall Father John could hear Father William snoring loudly. The sound was accompanied by the rhythmic squeak of Ignatius the hamster's wheel. Farther away, a train hooted morosely, and a bevy of neighborhood dogs began howling. He was fairly sure that one of them was Spot, reluctantly sequestered in the kitchen at night. Father John put down the beads and picked up his prayer book, thumbing through to the section entitled "The Office of the Dead."

"Like the deer that yearns for running streams, so my soul is yearning for you, my God," he prayed, in memory of Randall Ivy. It was the least that he could do.

* * *

When her doorbell rang, Francesca was stretched out

on her bedroom floor, doing exercises that were supposed to flatten the stomach. She jumped up from the floor and ran into the bathroom, where she quickly applied lipstick before heading to the door. She thought it might be Tony, and she hoped she didn't look too frowsy in her old jeans and sweater. But when she peeked through an opening in the door, she was surprised to see Thomas White from the choir. He was wearing a pale blue dress shirt and neatly pressed pants.

As she opened the door to let him in, he gave her a big smile. "I hope I'm not stopping by too early, but I was on my way to the university and thought I'd say hello. We're practically neighbors, you know."

"Oh, I didn't realize..." She returned his smile. "Someone else is covering phones at the rectory this morning, so I have a day off. Come in and have some coffee."

She deposited him on the sofa with a *National Geographic* magazine, right next to Tubs, who was snoring softly. Then she went into the kitchen to get the coffee pot. As she gathered up the mugs and joined him in the living room, she noticed that Tubs had awakened. He was purring while he gazed at Thomas. *A good sign.*

She put down the mugs on the coffee table, then went back into the kitchen to get the sugar bowl and cream. "So where do you live, Thomas?" she called from the kitchen.

"I moved into a house on Kathleen Drive, just three blocks away. I've been there about two weeks, and I've been meaning to stop by."

She didn't know much about Thomas, only that he was a tenor who'd joined the choir about the same time

Randall had become director.

She poured two mugs of coffee and handed him one. "Do you work nearby?"

"Actually, yes, I'm working on a master's degree in music at Emory." He took a sip of coffee.

"Oh, that sounds interesting." She was relieved that he wasn't in computers or business, which were usually conversation stoppers after the first few obvious remarks had been made.

"I'm getting a rather late start," he said. "You see, I spent my twenties and thirties doing the practical thing. I was in real estate. When I turned 40, I decided it was time to finally do what I loved. And that's music."

His turquoise-blue eyes roamed the living room, settling on the Celtic harp in the corner. "Do you play?"

"I'm afraid the extent of my musical ability is singing in the choir – and my greatest contribution is my talent at lip syncing," she joked. "The harp is, or rather was, my husband's. He could play just about any musical instrument by ear." She looked at the floor. "He…uh…he passed away."

Thomas put his coffee mug down on the table. "I'm sorry to hear that. When did it happen?"

"Two years ago. It was an automobile accident. A complete shock." There was something about the warm, understanding look in his eyes that made her feel as if she might start bawling. *Change the subject.*

"What do you think of the neighborhood so far?"

He glanced at his watch. "It's wonderful, lots of friendly people. And your coffee is excellent. I'm sorry I have to drink and run, but I have to get to class." Then he paused at the door. "I wonder: Would you like to go out for dinner some time?"

"That would be lovely."

Maybe the old adage about how it never rains but pours is really true. Could it be that all my prayers for a social life are being answered all at once?

"How about tomorrow night? I'll come by about six?"

"Sounds good." Then she added, "I guess I'll see you at rehearsal tonight." She'd already heard the rumor that Thomas would be filling in as director until a permanent person was hired.

After he left, she sat down on the couch by Tubs. "I think we're on a roll here."

Tubs meowed, and she realized it was treat time.

* * *

That evening, the choir members seemed unusually quiet as Francesca entered St. Rita's. It was their first rehearsal since Randall's death. Casting an appraising glance at the soprano section, she noticed that Lily looked pale and glum. Patricia, however, seemed as chipper as ever, dolled up in a powder-puff pink sweater with matching lipstick.

Thomas looked uncomfortable in front of the group. *Talk about a hard act to follow,* Francesca thought. Randall had been widely respected as a musician, and the choir was accustomed to his style.

"Let's say a prayer before we begin." Thomas cast his eyes downward and clasped his hands. "Heavenly Father, we thank you for bringing us together here tonight. We ask you to be with us during these difficult times and to guide us always toward your light. May your light shine on Randall's soul." His voice quavered a bit. "And may he rest in peace, amen."

"Amen," echoed the group.

An awkward silence followed until Bertha Chumley took out an economy-sized flowery handkerchief, dabbed her eyes, and let out a great honk. That seemed like the cue for the rest of the choir members to start talking to each other. Meanwhile, Patricia stood up and sashayed over to Thomas, batting her heavily painted eyelashes at him.

She emoted loudly. "I just want you to know, speaking for the whole choir, how pleased we are that you'll be taking over."

Francesca mentally rolled her eyes, while Rebecca poked her in the ribs and whispered: "I'll bet she's after him."

Rehearsal that night was a somewhat muted experience with few of the usual jokes. The choir went over "Very Bread," the anthem for Sunday. They also rehearsed a few more pieces for Christmas. Patricia didn't say a word about solos, nor did Lily or anyone else. When Patricia tripped awkwardly over a few measures in a way that would have infuriated Randall, Thomas winced but said nothing. And when he forgot to give the group their opening notes on one piece, he apologized profusely.

"Not to worry," chirped Patricia. "You'll get the hang of it in no time."

Rebecca turned to Francesca and whispered: "Methinks the lady doth not protest enough!"

Francesca drove home after choir practice, looking forward to a hot bath and a glass of wine before she went to bed. It was getting dark earlier and earlier. The sidewalks were slathered in piles of crunchy leaves, with just a few leaves left clinging tenaciously on the tree limbs. In the dark, the nearly bare branches had a spidery look. She felt chilly when she entered her house. *Better turn up the heat.*

But there was something else. She had an uneasy sense that she wasn't alone. *That's ridiculous; the front door was locked. And the back door too.*

Suddenly she remembered that earlier in the day she'd gone into the yard through the back door.

I did lock it, didn't I? Well, I'll just go check and be sure. Why am I so jumpy? That phone call really rattled me, I guess.

Once she was inside the house, she carefully locked the front door behind her and dropped the living room shades.

"Tubs, Tubs," she called out, but there was no sign of him. *That's strange; he's always here to greet me.*

Glancing into the guest room, she was startled to see Tubs crouching in the corner with the fur on his back raised ominously. She smelled an unpleasant sour aroma, but she couldn't quite place it.

It's almost like Tubs is afraid of someone, but there's no one...

Then she turned and saw a man standing in the hall. Her heart lurched in her chest. A chill snaked up her spine and she felt the tiny hairs on her arms standing up.

Oh, sweet St. Joseph, pray for me. Lord Jesus Christ,

Son of the living God, have mercy on me.

Suddenly she realized who the figure was, and her heart began racing at an even more frantic tempo. "What in the world are you doing here?" she gasped.

It was Scotty Brumble, looking every bit as sinister in his black leather and chains as he had when she'd first met him. But what happened next surprised her, because at the sound of her voice, Scotty took a step back. Despite his harrowing appearance, his facial expression was almost sheepish.

"Your back door was open, so I just came in. I was going to wait outside in the car, but you'd be amazed at how many people call the police on me just for the way I look."

She felt slightly nauseated from the waves of panic that were coursing through her body. He was so much bigger than she was, and stronger. *He's just stalling, and then he's going to attack me.*

Terrified of what he might do, she decided to try to distract him. With a huge effort, she attempted to make her voice sound normal, rather than terrified.

"Scotty, let's go into the living room where we can sit down and talk."

I have to act as if everything is just fine, she thought. *If he detects my panic, I'm done for.* He went into the living room and headed for the couch.

"How's your grandmother?" She was frantically searching for ways to divert his attention from whatever foul deed he was planning. She'd read somewhere that if you talked to a potential attacker there was a chance you might get him to change his mind.

"Oh, Granny's fine." He plopped down on the couch, his chains bumping together like empty tin cans. "She keeps busy, watching her soaps and her game shows."

She smiled widely, feigning great interest and approval, as if he'd just announced that Mrs. Brumble had been nominated for sainthood.

Scotty looked troubled. "Look, there's something you should know about Randall that the police don't know."

"Yes?" She stood up and edged nearer the door. "Listen, I'm going to crack the door to get some fresh air in here."

He didn't say anything, so she opened the front door wide. She was tempted to run outside and bang on a neighbor's door for help, but for some reason her fear of Scotty was rapidly dissipating. It was being replaced by an intense curiosity about what he might tell her.

Anyway, she comforted herself, *if he tries anything, I can get out easily.* She moved her chair closer to the door.

"You were saying? About Randall?"

"Look, when you live next to a guy a long time, you notice things. And I'm an observant kind of a guy. And there have been some very..." Here he stopped to pluck just the right word from his vocabulary bank. "Very seedy, yes, that's it, seedy-looking people going in and out of Randall's house some nights."

He paused now and delivered the jewel of information he'd come to hand her. "I think he was into some drugs, if you know what I mean."

And I wouldn't be at all surprised if I weren't staring right at his dealer, she thought cynically.

Scotty absently picked up a book from the coffee table.

He turned it over in his hand as if he were an archeologist examining an artifact from a lost civilization. It was a small hardbound edition of “The Imitation of Christ.” When he saw the title, he dropped the book as if it were radioactive. It fell with a resounding thud onto the tabletop.

He shifted on the couch and scratched his shaven head. “That’s all I came to say about Randall, but the main thing is not to bother my grandmother again. She’s got a heart condition and I don’t want no one upsetting her.”

“Of course, I understand. The only reason I asked her any questions at all was that I was concerned about Randall.”

“Well, it was suicide, plain and simple.” Scotty touched his nose ring as if to make sure it was still there. “See, my guess is Randall was into a lot of drugs, not just the stuff he killed himself with.” He shifted his weight and the chains rattled. “It’s just what happens.”

“I had nothing to do with his death,” he said firmly, as if reading her thoughts. Now his face assumed a sneer that reminded her of a particularly gruesome Halloween mask. “And I don’t want you – or anyone else -- snooping around in my life, understand?”

She nodded brightly, silently repeating her plea to Jesus for mercy. Scotty’s face relaxed, the sneering expression replaced by a blank look. He scratched his unshaven chin and continued.

“When you came to talk to Granny, I got suspicious. That stuff about checking out the neighborhood was pretty lame.”

So much for my acting career. “I suppose that’s why

you called me?"

He sniffed loudly and rubbed his nose against his sleeve. "I didn't call you. I came to see you in person. I knew where you lived because I followed you over here the other day."

She edged even closer to the open door, watching him nervously as he rose from the couch. He headed straight for the door.

"Well, I gotta go. Granny is waiting for me," he said as if they had just had a nice social chat. "This is our bowling night."

At that moment she didn't know which was more ludicrous: her mental picture of Mrs. Brumble in bowling shoes, trying to score a strike -- or the idea that Scotty really had nothing to do with Randall's death.

"And one more thing." He was outside now. Under the porch light, his numerous black tattoos gave him the appearance of someone who'd been badly burned in a fire.

"Yes?" She got a firm grip on the door so she could slam it in his face if necessary.

"You really should have better security around here." Then he clanked off into the night.

Her heart was still thumping ominously as she threw the deadbolt on the front door. Then she ran downstairs and locked the back door, silently condemning herself for being so careless earlier. She also checked all the windows. Meanwhile, Tubs had cautiously emerged from the bedroom and was standing in the kitchen, examining his empty supper dish. Francesca gave him an extra large portion of food and then poured herself a generous glass of wine.

What am I getting into here? She sank down on the couch. *Why don't I just take Tony's advice and keep out of it?*

The visit from Scotty had really shaken her. It could have been so much worse.

I'm exhausted and totally stressed out. I really should call Tony and tell him what happened, but all I want to do is sleep.

After finishing the wine, she checked the doors again, took a hot shower, and gathered up Tubs. Then she headed to bed. She slept that night with the lights on for good measure.

* * *

She overslept the next morning and arrived at the rectory a half hour late. Tony called just as she sat down at the desk. When she told him about the visit from Scotty, he sounded angry.

"I'm not angry with you, I'm furious with him. We can get him for breaking and entering."

She nervously toyed with a pencil. "Well, I'm ashamed to admit this, but somehow I left the back door unlocked."

There was a sigh on the other end. "We can still charge him with criminal trespassing."

She thought it over quickly. *If I bring charges against Scotty and for some reason they don't stick, he'll have even more reason to come after me. And he really didn't harm me, except for giving me a terrible scare.*

She bore down so hard with the pencil, she broke the lead. “I’m not sure I want to press charges. Maybe I’d rather just drop the whole thing.”

There was a pause on the other end of the line, then another big sigh. “It’s up to you, but if I were you, I’d get the guy. You never know what he might try next. Besides, I’m worried about you. Think it over, and let me know if you change your mind, OK?”

“Yes, Tony, I will.”

“You might as well know who you’re dealing with. I checked on Scotty in the computer, and he has a record. Nothing very serious: loitering, shoplifting, and one time for disturbing the peace.”

Tony seemed interested when she told him what Scotty had said about Randall and drugs, but he didn’t comment. At that moment, she noticed that Spot had entered the room and was sitting near her with what she took to be a longing expression on his face. He had carried in what appeared to be one of the priest’s slippers and apparently wanted her to throw it for him.

She ignored the dog. “From what Scotty said, it sounds like Randall could have been into the hard stuff. And isn’t it possible that Scotty was his dealer?” she postulated. “And what if Randall decided to get off drugs? And what if Scotty was afraid that Randall might tell the police who his dealer had been? And then Scotty decided to get rid of Randall?”

“The autopsy didn’t show any traces of drugs other than the legal prescriptions Randall was using,” Tony countered. “And we didn’t find anything when we searched his house.”

Now his tone of voice became very serious. “Francesca, I know you’re fascinated with what makes people tick, their motivations and all. But in this case, don’t play psychologist. It’s much too dangerous. If it’ll make you feel better, I’ll do some more checking on Scotty. But, remember, I’m doing this on my own time, since the case was ruled a suicide.”

“Tony, I want you to…STOP IT, right now!” she shouted.

“What do you mean?”

“Oh, not you, Tony, I’m talking to Spot, Father John’s dog. He’s trying to eat one of my shoes. Tony, I really appreciate what you’re doing. I promise to leave everything to you.”

After they said goodbye, she had to dissuade Spot from destroying her shoes. She also removed the slipper from his vicinity, placing it safely on the desk. As soon as her back was turned, however, he went for her purse. She removed it patiently from his drooling mouth and placed it out of harm’s way.

“Go get a toy.” He looked at her curiously. “Toy. Go. Get. A. Toy.” She carefully enunciated each word. He wagged his tail and vanished down the hall.

Margaret Hennessy appeared moments later, carrying a mug of coffee and wearing a yellow sweater and emerald-green pants. Somehow she reminded Francesca of a large parrot in her improbable colors, but a very friendly parrot. Margaret placed a Three Musketeers bar on the desk.

“A little sustenance. How are you, dear?”

Francesca almost broke down and told her about the visit from Scotty. But she was still embarrassed about having left her back door open.

"Just fine," she lied. There was the loud sound of toenails scraping against the wood floors, as Spot reappeared joyously in the foyer with something dangling from his mouth.

"What do you have, boy?" Francesca bent down and grabbed one end of the object in the dog's mouth and tugged. Spot appeared to be enjoying the game thoroughly, and surrendered his treasure with great reluctance. It was a pair of men's polka-dotted boxer shorts, now quite torn.

"Oh, my." Margaret's face had turned scarlet. "I bet that belongs to one of the priests."

At that moment, Francesca saw Father William, prayer book in hand, coming down the hall. At this time of morning, she knew he was probably on his way to visit elderly patients at the Eternal Sunrise Nursing Home. After that, he usually headed over to Emory Hospital to give Communion to Catholic patients. She had often heard him say that it was his favorite part of being a priest, comforting the sick and lonely.

"I'm off to do my visits," he announced to the two women. Then his face turned a more vivid shade than Margaret's.

"Uh, Father, it seems Spot somehow got hold of..." Somehow Francesca was unable to say "underwear" in front of him.

The dog spared them the embarrassment of any further discussion by suddenly lifting his leg and watering the carpet. In the ensuing chaos, the boxer shorts were forgotten.

Chapter 8

The voice on the telephone the next morning sounded tentative and nervous. And when the caller identified herself as Lily, Francesca was surprised.

Now what? I've promised Tony to leave the case to him. Still, I shouldn't jump to conclusions. Maybe this call has nothing to do with Randall's death.

"I've meant to call you sooner." Lily's vowels revealed traces of her native Spanish. "There are some things I'd like to talk to you about, but not over the phone. Can you stop by for coffee – maybe this morning?"

It turned out that Lily's place wasn't that far from Randall's, so it took Francesca only a few minutes to drive there. The house immediately brought to mind the word "charming" with all the associated clichés. It was adorned with an almost preternaturally manicured yard.

The driveway was gleaming white, and there was not a leaf out of place. Francesca thought about her own yard, usually strewn with leaves, bread crumbs, and the occasional pile of poop from the neighbor's dog, Bainbridge. As she rang the doorbell, she looked around, half expecting to see a well-groomed squirrel decked out in a tuxedo.

Lily was attired in a pair of black corduroy pants and a long-sleeved purple sweater that exactly matched the stones in her earrings. Her big dark eyes were carefully circled in black liner, and her lips were the color of blackberries. She invited Francesca to sit down on a flower-print couch in the living room.

"I'll be right back," Lily said. "The muffins are almost ready."

Homemade muffins. Francesca savored the aroma. *I didn't realize Lily was so domestic.*

She settled back on the couch, which was almost groaning under the weight of ruffles. Then, glancing around the living room, she recognized the unmistakable signs of a devoted disciple of Martha Stewart. A cluster of hand-decorated knick-knacks perched upon the mantle, while on a nearby shelf, picture frames were adorned with shells and dried flowers.

She had long been convinced that, just as wild animals can be identified by their droppings, Martha Stewart's followers make their presence known with a trail of glitter, ruffles, and artificial flowers.

Once she'd read an article by Martha describing how to make party favors out of egg shells. First you had to remove the raw eggs from the shells, which was a miraculous enough feat. Then you had to glue diminutive, dried flowers inside the shells. It had sounded like an abominable waste of eggs and time, she recalled.

Or maybe I just have a case of sour grapes because every time I try to make something by hand, it looks like an infant did it.

Lily emerged from the kitchen carrying a shining tray upon which rested an engraved silver coffee pot and delicate china cups with a butterfly motif. Cream and sugar were cozily ensconced in matching china vessels, and a cluster of steaming muffins perched upon a platter.

Lily carefully handed Francesca a cup of coffee and placed a muffin on a china plate, along with a generous slab of butter. Then Lily poured herself a cup of coffee and sat down in the ruffled chair opposite Francesca. An unusual spicy odor, which was emanating from a bowl on the table, wafted up to Francesca's nostrils. *Potpourri, another sure sign of Martha.*

The tender muffin was delicious and the butter oozed generously over its top, coating Francesca's fingers with a sweet slickness. As they sipped the steaming coffee, which Lily said was made from freshly ground beans, Francesca murmured a few sincere compliments about the muffins. And then Lily launched right in.

"Well, I don't want to beat around the proverbial bush, so I'll just come right out with it."

"Mmm?" Francesca's mouth was too full of muffin to say much else.

"I think you've figured out that Candy is my daughter, haven't you?"

Francesca didn't know if she should feign surprise or just admit the truth. Since her mouth was too full to do much feigning, she nodded, and then felt a slow blush creeping into her cheeks.

"How did you know?" she asked, although it sounded more like: "Mow did do doh?" thanks to the muffin.

Lily picked up a perfectly ironed cloth napkin and touched it to her lips. "Oh, Candy said she saw you in the restaurant when you were out with that police officer. She thought you were eavesdropping on us."

"Eavesdropping! I was just standing by the cashier, and you both were talking so loud, I couldn't help but hear."

Lily said nothing while refilling their coffee cups.

"In any event, there's a lot more to the story. You see, Randall and I were married for only three years. It was a very unhappy marriage, to put it mildly. He started cheating on me after the first year, and it just went from bad to worse. He was always very apologetic when I found out, and he would promise it would never happen again."

Lily toyed absently with her muffin, while Francesca chewed quietly and listened.

"It's like the alcoholic who promises he'll get on the wagon tomorrow. Tomorrow just never comes. We had Candy at the end of the first year we were married. I made up my mind I'd do whatever it took to keep the marriage intact." She sighed. "So I stayed with him two more years and pretended everything was fine."

Just then, a snow-white miniature poodle entered the room. The dog had little pink ribbons attached to the fur on its ears, plus toenails that looked freshly painted. Lily scooped up the little dog and gave it a kiss on its pristine head.

"This is Snowflake." Her tone softened just a bit.

Francesca gave the dog a gentle pat on the head. She could tell this was a dog that would never shed, bark out of turn, or eat someone's boxer shorts. This was a Martha Stewart dog.

"You can probably imagine how hard it was." Lily readjusted the dog's hair bows. "I was constantly suspicious of him. And my self-esteem was pretty low. I guess on some level I figured he wouldn't have been such a playboy if I had been a better wife."

Francesca sipped her coffee thoughtfully, uncertain of how to respond. Then she realized she didn't have to say anything; Lily was so intent on unraveling her tale that she didn't need input from her audience.

"When it became too much for me to take, I divorced him. He moved to Decatur a few years later to start a new life, and I only heard from him occasionally. I had the definite impression he didn't really change his wild ways. But I never bad-mouthed him in front of Candy. You see, I wanted her to grow up admiring her father."

Lily's ploy seems to have worked, Francesca mused. Candy had seemed fairly star-struck when talking about Randall.

Lily put Snowflake on the floor, and the dog curled up on the spotless white carpet and fell asleep.

"Then, ironically enough, my singing career brought me and Candy to Decatur. When I joined St. Rita's about five years ago, I felt right at home." She made a little grimace. "But he wasn't the choir director then -- and you can imagine my surprise when he was hired."

Her mouth was set in a determined way. "I decided not to let him ruin our lives. I liked the church and the choir, so I wasn't about to leave."

Francesca helped herself to a second muffin. *Delicious and a lot healthier than donuts, I'm sure,* she told her conscience.

"Well, he and I had a long talk. We both wanted to put the past behind us, so we decided not to tell everyone about our former relationship. As for Candy, he'd never been much of a father to her, so the three of us just agreed to keep the whole thing quiet."

A little flicker of distaste shot over her face. "I guess we were all living one big lie," she said bitterly. "A few months ago, I started dating someone else. I really felt there was a chance for a future with this guy. Then, out of the blue, Randall started coming on to me again, just like in the early days when we were dating. Told me he'd changed his ways and wanted me back."

Lily let out a big sigh, and Snowflake opened an eye and stared at her. "He said what I wanted to hear. How he'd really matured and changed -- and he wanted us to remarry."

She paused and refilled their coffee cups. "I wanted Randall, so I broke up with the guy I was dating."

Now she fiddled nervously with the cloth napkin on her lap. "It wasn't long before Randall started down the same old path again." She uttered the next words as if reciting a litany: "Pursuits, conquests, deception, regrets."

Francesca hoped she didn't have a guilty look on her face. *I guess I was one of the pursuits, and Lily probably thinks I was a conquest too.*

"Now that I look back, I think what Randall wanted all along was to be sure I didn't get involved with anyone else."

Lily really has a lot of reasons to hate him. It sounds like he treated her like dirt. "Were you one of the women who visited him after the party that night?" She figured it was time for her to wade into Lily's stream of consciousness.

Lily looked startled: "Women? I thought Patricia was the only one?"

"Well, I don't know how accurate this piece of information is, but one of his neighbors said she saw *two* women visiting him that night."

Lily glanced at her well-manicured fingernails. "More coffee?" She lifted the silver pot. Its thin spout exhaled a delicate sliver of steam.

"Sure." *Lily's stalling for time.*

"I didn't go to see him that night," Lily said. "I was so fed up with him after the party, I just went home." Her voice quavered. "I wish I had gone, though, because maybe I could have prevented him from...from..."

She pressed her hand to her mouth and looked as if she would cry. "You see, Francesca, despite all our arguments and all his running around, I still loved him. I never stopped."

Lily idly plucked a faded petal from a peach-colored rose in the crystal vase on the coffee table. As she did, four other petals suddenly took a nosedive.

I wonder if she's telling the truth, Francesca mused. *After all, as a professional singer, Lily is trained in projecting a wide range of emotions at will. But maybe I'm being overly suspicious.*

Lily cleared her throat nervously. "There's something I want to ask you. Do you have his love letters and his journal?" Her eyes indicated that she knew the answer.

"Love letters and journal?" Francesca hoped she sounded innocent. *If Lily can read expressions, then mine is shouting "Yes, I do."*

"When we were on good terms, Randall mentioned that his latest flame had sent him numerous love letters. And Randall was a pack rat, so I know he would have kept them. I also know he kept a journal."

Lily paused. "But when I looked through his house, they were gone."

Francesca took elaborate care in folding the napkin and placing it back on the table.

"Why would you think I might have them?"

"Well, I know you had access to his office. And Candy mentioned that you had a box of his stuff." Here she shot Francesca an accusing look.

What's the point of hiding anything? "I did find the letters and his journal in his office. I'm sure he didn't realize they were there, and I would have given them to him immediately if he…he were still alive. But I didn't want to give them to Candy because I wasn't sure he would want *her* to have them. Plus, they could have had some important evidence in them."

"Evidence?" Lily put down the coffee cup with such force that Francesca was surprised it didn't shatter. "What do you mean?"

Might as well drop the bombshell. "I've had this very uncomfortable feeling, right from the start, that Randall's death wasn't a suicide."

Lily stared at her with an expression Francesca couldn't quite place. Fear? Worry?

"I think someone killed him," Francesca said evenly.

Lily's hand shot up to her mouth, and her eyes seemed to double in size. She reached down and picked up the little dog, holding it against her like a teddy bear.

Either she's a wonderful actress, Francesca thought, *or she's really never considered this possibility.*

"Killed?" Lily gasped. "No, that's impossible. No one

would do something like that to him." She nervously stroked Snowflake.

"He was depressed," Lily continued. "And he was drunk and had the medicine handy." She wet her lips nervously. "He'd tried it before."

"Oh?" This was news to Francesca, and she was definitely interested in hearing more. If what Lily was saying was true, then maybe it really was time to take Tony's advice and consider the case closed.

"Yes, he attempted suicide before," Lily repeated, as if answering the look of disbelief in Francesca's eyes. "Years ago. He drank too much wine and downed a bottle of antidepressants. I got there in time and took him to a hospital. He had his stomach pumped."

Francesca mulled over this piece of information. It would be easy to conclude that because he had tried it once and failed, therefore this time had really been suicide. But she had studied enough logical propositions during her philosophy days to know this conclusion might be false.

Lily began pacing now. The question about the love letters lingered in the air like smoke from a grease fire.

"Where are they? Where are the letters and the journal now?"

"I gave them to Tony Viscardi, the investigator you saw me with at the restaurant."

"*Mierda*!" Lily reverted to Spanish in her anger. Perspiration had broken out on her face. "How could you do that? How could you?"

Lily continued pacing nervously, while Snowflake glanced at Francesca and let out a little growl. "Why couldn't you just keep your nose out of our business? Those were personal things, and you had no right to take them. You had no right to give them to anyone." She clenched her fists. "Oh, I'm just furious!"

Now I'm really in it knee deep, Francesca thought. *Maybe I should have expected this temper tantrum.*

"Why are they so important to you?" she asked.

"Because I believe they have information in them that I never want my daughter to know about her father, that's why. And I wanted to destroy them."

"What kind of information?"

Lily laughed, but it sounded more like one of Snowflake's growls. "Do you really think I'm going to tell you that? Why should I trust you?"

Francesca decided it was time to exit. She placed the china cup and saucer carefully back on the silver tray. Then she stood up, moving as far away from Snowflake as possible.

"Well, it's been lovely, Lily, but I have to go. I, er, I have another appointment."

Lily simply stood there glaring at her as she left. *Definitely not a Martha Stewart farewell,* Francesca thought, hurrying down the well-kept path to her car.

* * *

As she drove home, she mulled over the things she had learned. Lily and Randall had shared a very stormy past filled with recriminations and broken promises. And Lily had somehow managed to paint a pretty rosy picture of the man to their daughter. But what if Randall had become such a bother to Lily that in a moment of anger she had decided to end the whole charade?

Lily could have written those letters herself. And now she's afraid that information about their stormy relationship will leak out. Information that might somehow link her to the crime, as well as tarnish Candy's radiant image of her dad.

Still deep in thought, Francesca decided to stop at a nearby shopping center to pick up some pizza for lunch. *Instead of getting a whole pizza, I'll just get two slices. This way, I won't be tempted to overeat.*

Her plan was to eat lunch at home, but the hot pizza was so tempting, she started devouring a slice on the way to her car. She stopped briefly in the parking lot and tossed a paper napkin into the trash bin.

"HAVE A WONDERFUL DAY" a woman's voice chortled as the trash can lid opened. *Oh, no, talking trash cans. I just hope the toilet bowl industry doesn't jump on the bandwagon.*

As she was climbing into her car, she spotted a familiar figure standing by a small boutique. The woman was staring at a black velvet evening dress in the window. It was Patricia weighted down with numerous bags and shoeboxes, evidence of a serious shopping spree. Francesca hailed her and walked over. *I hope I don't have pizza smudges on my face.*

"Oh, Francesca! You'll never believe what I found."

Patricia unearthed a chunky glittering bracelet from one of the bags and held it up for Francesca to admire. "Isn't it just the most beautiful thing you've ever seen? It was very pricey, but you know what Oprah always says."

"Uh, actually, no, I don't think I do." *Here it comes, the prosperity gospel according to Oprah Winfrey.*

"Why, she always says that we should treat ourselves because we are worth it! We deserve to have the best. Haven't you ever heard that philosophy?"

"Well, I guess if you can afford it…"

Patricia winced. "Oh, Francesca, don't you see? If you treat yourself to nice things, the universe will smile on you, and you will be given even nicer things." She cradled the bracelet in her hands. "By the way, I think you have a pizza smudge on your face."

"Let me show you the earrings I also found." Patricia juggled her bags awkwardly.

Shopping must be women's version of hunting, Francesca thought. *And heaven knows I'm familiar with the sport: spotting the prey, bagging it, and then displaying it proudly.*

Suddenly one of Patricia's bags fell from her arms and hit the pavement. Something made of glass broke and splattered liquid all over the sidewalk. An acrid aroma reached Francesca's nostrils as she and Patricia attempted to clean up the broken glass. And then she caught a glimpse of the label on the bottle: a very expensive brand of Scotch.

"I didn't know you were a Scotch drinker," Francesca commented.

"Oh, not really, but I like to keep my liquor cabinet well-stocked. For guests, you know."

* * *

Arriving home, she thought about the incident again. *Patricia had seemed unusually flustered by what had happened. But maybe it's because she's a secret drinker and doesn't want anyone to know. I'd better not start psychoanalyzing her.*

She was glad she had accepted the date with Thomas, even though part of her wished she were getting ready to see Tony. She found it somewhat odd how quickly she had bonded emotionally with Tony, and how attracted she was to him. But she also knew the dangers of becoming attached to a man she didn't really know that well. She needed to divert her romantic energy. Going out with Thomas seemed a perfect solution to the problem of falling too quickly for Tony.

As she was dressing, Tony called. "I think you'll be pleased with my news. You won't have to worry about any more threatening phone calls or visits from Scotty. We've arrested him for drug dealing."

"Oh?" She was somewhat startled, and just the slightest bit sad as well. It might be true that Scotty was a drug dealer, but he was young and there was something pathetic about him. No doubt he'd grow even harder and meaner behind bars. And she couldn't help but wonder what would happen to his grandmother now.

"We sent an undercover man to one of the places Brumble frequents regularly," Tony continued. "It didn't take long before Brumble approached the guy and tried to make a deal with him. Brumble's dealing in some serious stuff – heroin and cocaine and pills."

"Well, it's a relief to know he won't be dropping by here any longer," Francesca admitted.

She could hear the smile in Tony's voice. "I thought you'd be pleased."

Then he asked about her day and Francesca told him about visiting Lily. She also told him about dropping by the shopping center. When she mentioned Patricia and the broken Scotch bottle, he laughed heartily.

"Sounds like she doesn't want people to know she's drinking more than just a glass of white wine now and again."

"That's probably it."

Tony invited her to dinner that night, but she had to turn him down because of her date with Thomas. She didn't share the details, just that she was "busy."

"Well, maybe we can try again another night. Next time I'll be sure to ask you earlier. Take care and I'll talk to you soon."

She sighed as she hung up the phone. *I'd rather be going out with Tony tonight.*

* * *

Thomas and Francesca ended up at a small French restaurant on the square in downtown Decatur, two doors down from the Italian place. The waitress was a twentyish French woman who resembled the young Katherine Hepburn. She was so refined and elegantly made up that she made Francesca feel slightly out of place. In some ways, Francesca almost missed the waitress with the tattoos and nose ring. At least she didn't put on airs.

Thomas seemed familiar with the French dishes, and he recommended the salmon in butter and cream sauce very highly, so Francesca decided to try it. He also ordered a delicious Chardonnay, which she suspected was very expensive.

The appetizers, clumps of crabmeat and asparagus drenched in butter sauce, were delicious, although the conversation was somewhat strained. Thomas liked to talk about classical music, and Francesca, whose tastes ran more to jazz and country-Western, didn't know a lot of the pieces he was referring to. So she simply nodded her head pleasantly. After a while, she began to get a crick in her neck.

Just as their entrees arrived, she looked up and saw something that doubled the ache in her neck almost instantly. It was Tony, looking dashing and desirable, and on his arm was none other than the stately Lily. She was adorned in a drop-dead beautiful, low-cut dress that left little to the imagination. Francesca's first impulse was to hide. She tried to shift over in her seat so she'd be partially blocked from their view by Thomas. But it didn't work. Lily and Tony hailed her and headed over to the table.

"Hello, Francesca. Hi, Thomas," Lily drawled sweetly. "What a surprise seeing you both here."

Lily gave Thomas a particularly appraising look. *Maybe Lily thinks I'm buttering him up for a solo*, Francesca thought cynically. Her spirits rose a bit when she noticed that Tony looked just a bit guilty. But then she quickly chastised herself: *This is ridiculous; we're not married.*

"How nice to see you both," she lied and then introduced the men to each other. "Tony, this is Thomas

White, who's also in the choir at St. Rita's. Thomas, this is Inspector Tony Viscardi from the Decatur police station."

"Oh, a man of the law," Thomas said, laughing. "Shouldn't you be out patrolling the streets to make them safer for citizens?"

"They gave me some time off – for good behavior," Tony commented drily.

Francesca watched as Lily and Tony headed back to their table. *Was it my imagination or did Tony give Thomas a particularly intense once over? Maybe he's jealous. Or maybe I'm projecting*, she thought glumly, for when she heard Lily's sparkling laughter moments later, she felt very jealous herself.

After the meal, Thomas invited her back to his house for coffee and an after-dinner drink. She was tired and longing to go home and spend time with Tubs and a good book. But she figured it would be just for an hour, so she agreed. She'd already crossed him off her future dating list during the meal; they just didn't seem to share that much in common.

Thomas lived in a sprawling two-story house on Kathleen Drive, which was also located in Chelsea Heights. The plush furnishings rather surprised Francesca, who had been expecting bare-bones, graduate-student decor. Then she remembered he had told her about having been in real estate. *He's probably fairly well-off*, she thought, settling down on the white couch in his living room. Once he'd started a fire in the fireplace, the topic turned to Randall.

"I just can't believe it was suicide," she said, as they

sat sipping their coffee.

"But didn't the police rule it *was* suicide and drop the case?" Thomas wondered.

She added more cream to her coffee and took another sip. "Yes, they did, but all the pieces don't add up in my mind. I still think there was some kind of foul play. Call it woman's intuition."

Thomas walked across the room and adjusted the volume on the CD player. "I think you'll like this. It's 'Depuis le jour,' a really beautiful piece."

Then he sat beside her, rather close, she noted, and smiled. "Well, Mrs. Bibbo, tell me your theories. Who do you think did it?"

She smiled too. The music was pleasant, and the flames were dancing around in the fireplace very dramatically. *Maybe he's not that bad after all.* She made herself more comfortable on the couch.

She nodded when he brought the coffee pot near her cup, and he refilled it. "I can tell you the suspects. Father John, Lily, Candy, Patricia – or one of Randall's neighbors, Scotty Brumble – or someone else, someone we don't know."

"Father John?" Thomas exclaimed with a laugh. "And Lily and Patricia? I can't imagine any of them harming a fly, can you?"

She chuckled. "Not really. Truth be told, my woman's intuition isn't always completely reliable."

"And who's Candy?"

The wine had definitely loosened her tongue. Before she could stop herself, she told him about the secret tie that connected Randall, Candy, and Lily.

"Well, still waters do run deep," he mused. "Sounds like our choir director had quite an interesting life, unbeknownst to any of us."

Then he took her hand. "But that's all in the past. Let's celebrate our first date by having a glass of port. I have a bottle in the basement that I've been saving for a special occasion. We can have it with some cheddar cheese."

One more glass of anything, and I'm likely to fall off the couch. I'd better be careful. And then she thought of Tony wining and dining Lily, and she felt a stab of bitter jealousy. *I bet the two of them are strolling along in downtown Decatur, arm in arm, just enjoying themselves to no end.*

"Sure, why not?"

I'm not that drunk. And anyway the cheddar will absorb some of the alcohol.

While he went downstairs to get the port, she nestled up on the couch and watched the fire. Then she noticed a few notebooks stacked neatly on the coffee table in front of her. *I wonder what kind of lectures on music they give in graduate school.* She began flipping through one of the notebooks.

There were names of composers and musical selections, facts about operas, plus critical comments made by the professor. *Another world to me.* She yawned. At that moment, she heard Thomas coming back up the stairs.

"I'm going to open the port in the kitchen and let it breathe. And I'll get some cheese and crackers for us. Are you doing alright?"

"Just fine. The fire is lovely, and so is the music."

She leaned back on the couch and studied a few of the oil paintings in the living room. *He has good taste. The furniture isn't ostentatious, but it's a nice quality.*

He came back into the living room and put a platter of cheese and crackers on the coffee table. He also handed her a glass of port. Just then, she felt an odd clutching feeling in the pit of her stomach. It was an empty, lonely sensation like she used to have when she was very young and her mother left her with a babysitter.

Now what is this all about? He sat beside her and they toasted with the port. When he put his arm around her shoulders, she suddenly felt her heart lurch.

Oh, dear Lord! The handwriting in the notebook looks like the handwriting in the love letters.

Chapter 9

Lily's invitation for an after-dinner drink at her place was somewhat tempting, but Tony decided to turn her down. She was an attractive woman, especially in that dress, but he wasn't interested in what else she might be offering. It wasn't very creative, but he had used the first excuse that came to mind. Work was waiting for him at the office.

When she heard that, Lily's bright expression had dimmed considerably, but he shrugged it off mentally. After all, he hadn't invited her out to start with. She had called him earlier that day. She said she wanted to talk with him. She had also suggested the French restaurant and insisted on picking up the tab.

While they were eating their appetizers, she had told him point blank what she wanted.

"I heard through the…er…grapevine that you have some of Randall's letters and his journal. I think they belong to the family. I want them. After all, even if we were divorced, he was still the father of my only child."

"And did you write the letters?" He had decided to cut to the chase.

"I didn't write them and if you check the handwriting, you'll know I'm telling the truth." The big dark eyes had flashed with annoyance.

He had stalled for time by buttering his roll. He wanted to annoy her a bit, because she might be more inclined to blurt out the truth. "Who did write them then?"

"I have no idea." But the expression in her eyes had hinted otherwise.

"Look, Lily, I'll give you the journal and letters, but not until I've thoroughly looked them over. Even though the case is closed, I'm starting to have some doubts about it."

"Doubts?"

"It's just a hunch, but I have to follow it. It's possible it wasn't a suicide at all."

She had licked her lips nervously. "You must have been talking with Francesca. She seems to have this weird theory that Randall was murdered. But it's crazy, and I wish you would get her to stop meddling in the case!"

"Maybe it is crazy, but, as I said, I'd rather follow the hunch. And as for Francesca, I can't stop her. It's a free country, as they say, and she isn't breaking any law that I know of."

Lily had sighed dramatically and looked very pained.

When Tony and Lily left the restaurant, Thomas and Francesca were still there. Tony had glanced over at their table a few times, noticing that Francesca wasn't saying much but seemed quite intent on listening to Thomas.

I wonder what's up with them. And then he was surprised by his next thought: *I hope it isn't anything serious.*

When he got to Lily's house, she came up with a rather creative way to get him inside.

"Oh, that's my little Snowflake, barking. She only does that if she thinks there's an intruder. Wouldn't you just come in for a moment to make sure everything is OK?" As Lily spoke, the scent of her cologne, heavy and musky, wafted toward him.

Now Tony couldn't turn her down. He was, after all, a police officer, and he would never forgive himself if he failed to protect a woman who was in danger.

"Well, I can't stay long, but I'll come in and take a quick look around." He glanced at his watch to drive home the point.

Once inside the house, they discovered Snowflake barking at a moth that she was chasing around the room. *Is it my imagination or does Lily look disappointed? Maybe she hoped for something more dramatic so I'd stick around longer.*

"Well, I'm glad there was nothing to worry about. And thank you again for the meal." He made his way quickly to the door, relieved to be getting out so soon.

Lily's nice, he thought, as he pulled out of her driveway, *but really not my type.* He liked women who were a little less polished and sophisticated. He had cringed when he saw all the ruffles on her furniture, and the distinctive aroma of some kind of potpourri. He hated ruffles and scented candles and all that stuff. They reminded him of Martha Stewart, whom one of his aunts worshiped.

Every time he visited Aunt Louise, she was poring over Martha's magazines. Aunt Louise's house was crammed with herds of cutesy knickknacks and fussy flower arrangements that got on his nerves. It took her hours to dust everything, and by the time she was through, she had to start over again. It just didn't make sense to him.

He liked Francesca's house because it was fairly low key, nothing fancy, and he'd noticed plenty of things that needed repairs. There was something touching and slightly needy about her, which he also liked. Unlike so many women he'd dated, Francesca's life had loose ends that a man could enjoy tying up.

When he'd noticed the gutters of her house overflowing with leaves, his first instinct had been to climb up on the roof and get to work. The yard needed tending, and some of the rooms could have used a coat of paint. In his estimation, the trouble with so many single women was that they didn't seem to have room for a man in their lives. They had careers, they had expensive cars, and they had big houses with all the trimmings. Even though many of them claimed to be looking for a husband, a man seemed like an afterthought.

So much for dime-store philosophy, he mused, turning on the radio. *Maybe I should take some college courses in philosophy like Francesca did.* But then a block later, he switched the radio off. There was a doubt nagging at the back of his mind, and it was making him uneasy.

Something about White rubbed me the wrong way. I'm probably a little jealous, but I think it's more than that. It was the way he immediately had to make a joke about the police keeping the streets safe.

Over the years, Tony had learned that people who were quick to poke fun at his profession often did so because they had something to hide. He also had learned to trust his hunches, so he decided to run by the station in Decatur and run a computer check on White's background.

He needed White's birth date and address, so he made a quick call to St. Rita's rectory. He asked the woman answering the phone that evening to look through the church records. Luckily she wasn't the suspicious type who might have refused to give out information over the phone. She gave him White's birth date, along with his current Decatur address and an address where he'd previously lived.

After he'd entered the information on Thomas White into the computer, Tony grabbed a cup of coffee from the pot in the station. *Abysmal as usual*, he thought, taking a sip of the bitter liquid.

A few seconds later, he put down the coffee cup. He sat ramrod straight at the desk, reading the information on the screen.

* * *

Francesca was experiencing an uncomfortable mixture of emotions. Her rational mind said her suspicions were unfounded; it was just a coincidence. But in her heart she felt a growing dark cloud of doubt.

"A penny for your thoughts." Thomas moved a bit closer.

"Oh, they're not worth that much." She hoped her emotional turmoil wasn't showing on her face. Then she put down her glass with an air of finality. "I think I'd like to go home now."

His face fell. *This is stupid. He's going out of his way to be a good host and I'm acting idiotic.*

"Is it the port? Don't you like it?"

"It's delicious, but I feel so tired. I need to get some sleep."

And she realized it was true. She felt so drowsy from all the alcoholic beverages that she could hardly keep her head up. *And, even if I'm being idiotic, I want to go home. I want to put on my comfy cow pajamas and snuggle up to Tubs.*

In moments, Thomas' disappointment seemed to intensify into a sulky, childish attitude. He put down his glass, stood up, and began pacing. When he turned to speak to her, his mood had changed again. She was startled to realize that he was quite angry.

"Oh, why don't you just say it?" he spat. "Just say you don't like me. And you don't want to go to bed with me. You don't have to make up excuses."

"I'm not making up excuses." She was more confused than ever now. *Why is he talking about going to bed with me? Does he just assume that's part of the evening's agenda? And why is he acting so infantile?*

"Were you and Randall friends?" *Maybe if I can get him to talk about Randall, I can figure out if he wrote the letters. Maybe it's just some very weird coincidence about the handwriting.*

"Friends?" His laugh sounded like a bark. "Yes, you might say that. We were very close, and we spent a lot of time together. We both loved music and we both wanted to devote our lives to it. But Randall kept getting sidetracked."

He ran his fingers nervously through his hair. He took a gulp of the port. He looked distraught.

"Look, I hope this won't shock you too terribly," Thomas blurted out, "but Randall and I were lovers."

"Lovers?" she echoed incredulously.

"Yes, lovers, as in soul mates, partners, significant others, whatever else you want to call it."

"Oh, I didn't realize. I thought he was...that is, I didn't know he was, er, gay."

Now the script started going in a direction that she would never have envisioned.

"Who said anything about gay? Randall was bisexual. So am I." He pronounced the word almost proudly, as if he were revealing his allegiance to an esoteric religious sect.

"You've heard of bisexuals, haven't you?" His voice was ringing with angry sarcasm.

Things are getting too strange here, she thought, *I've got to go home.*

"Listen, Thomas, I really..." she started to say, but he interrupted.

"I know what you're going to say," he hissed angrily. He stalked across the room and grabbed her by the arm. He started pulling her roughly from the couch. "You're tired, you have a headache, and you want to go home. The truth is, you don't want to go out with a weirdo, isn't that right?"

"No, that's not it at all." She struggled against him. But he was strong and he jerked her toward him, and then he kissed her so hard that her lips started to bleed.

"Thomas, for God's sake, what are you doing?" she screamed, as she felt his hands grabbing roughly at her sweater. "Get away from me!"

Somehow she managed to break free and started running for the door.

This must be a nightmare. I must be asleep. I've been stuck in dreams before, and screaming made me wake up. But it isn't working now.

* * *

Tony read the information on White quickly, his mind absorbing the puzzle pieces and putting them together as he read. White had been picked up six years ago for beating up a live-in girlfriend. She had dropped the charges, so nothing had come of it. He'd been picked up another time for indecent exposure, but he'd gotten out on some technicality.

Tony checked the dispatcher's files to see if neighbors had lodged complaints against White at either his current or previous address. *Bingo,* he thought, as he discovered an entry with White's former address on it. A Decatur police officer, Roger Spalding, had been dispatched a year ago to White's house. It seems the neighbors had telephoned the police department to complain about a raucous party.

The city of Decatur wasn't known for wild parties, and complaints were few and far between. So Tony figured there was a good chance that the officer who'd been dispatched would remember the event. He dialed Roger Spalding's extension.

"Hey, it's Tony. This is a long shot, but how good is your memory?"

"Pretty decent. Whaddya need?"

Tony explained about the party and gave Spalding the exact date and address. Tony heard Spalding chuckling.

"Oh, yeah, I remember that party, you can bet your bottom dollar on that. See, it's not often you see a party like the one White was hosting that night. Well, maybe in the French Quarter..."

"Meaning what?" Tony wanted Spalding to get to the point quickly.

Tony could hear him taking a drag from his cigarette. "It's the only party I ever saw where the chicks were really guys."

"You mean drag queens?" Tony shot back, simultaneously grabbing his car keys and rising from his chair.

"You got it, buddy."

* * *

Francesca couldn't seem to extricate herself from the nightmare. Thomas stopped her as she tried to get out his front door. But he wasn't playing rough anymore. He took her gently by the hand as if they were a couple at a party on their way to the dance floor. She noticed that his mood had changed again. And somehow this was even more frightening because she didn't know what would come next.

"Look, I don't want to hurt you, so let's just calm down." He extracted a clean handkerchief from his pocket and gave it to her. She clutched it against her lips.

"I'm sorry for hurting you, I really am. I had too much to drink. Let me take you home."

Francesca was now trembling from head to foot. She wanted to believe he was having a change of heart, but she didn't trust him. She decided to play it safe. *I'll go along with whatever he says. I'll act like nothing unusual has happened. If I can just get home safely, everything will be fine.* She kept seeing an image of Tubs at home waiting for her. She tried flashing Thomas a smile, hoping it didn't look too much like a grimace.

"Yes, Thomas, why don't you take me home?" She tried to assume a normal tone of voice. "We've had a long evening and a lot to drink. I think we both need some rest."

He helped her into her jacket, and they stepped outside. He opened the car door for her, and she slipped inside as if nothing had happened. It was only a short drive to her house. She was silent in the car, but her mind was racing.

I don't want this guy in my house, so I'll have to act quickly when we get there. If I see someone on the street, I'll start screaming or make a big scene. I'll yell something about calling the police.

But as they drove down her street, she noted with desperation that it was deserted. She could see lights flickering in many of the windows. *All my neighbors are sealed inside their houses, watching TV. Even if I start screaming, they wouldn't hear me.*

She did the only thing she knew to do under the circumstances. She prayed. *Lord Jesus Christ, Son of the living God, have mercy on me. N*ext she petitioned St. Joseph, as she always had as a child. *Holy St. Joseph, pray for me; please help me.*

Then she said the prayer that had comforted her since childhood, when she had first held rosary beads in her hands.

"Hail Mary, full of grace, the Lord is with thee, blessed art thou among women, and blessed is the fruit of thy womb, Jesus. Holy Mary, Mother of God, pray for us sinners now and at the hour of our death. Amen."

For the first time, the closing words probed painfully at a deep place in her heart. *Is this the hour of my death?*

Chapter 10

As Thomas was parking the car in her driveway, Francesca saw her chance. As soon as he opens his door and gets out, I'll jump out and make a run for it. But her hands were shaking as she fumbled with her seatbelt, and Thomas was out of the car and at her side before she could undo it. Without a word, he released her seatbelt, then grasped her arm in a very firm and determined way. She realized there was no chance of escaping. And unless she thought of something very quickly, it was clear that he planned to accompany her inside her house.

"I want to come in for a few minutes and explain." His tone of voice was apologetic as he helped her out of the car. "I really need someone to talk to."

"I don't think it's a good idea, Thomas. It's been a long evening and I'm exhausted." She could tell her voice had a frantic edge to it, despite her attempt to keep calm.

His grip tightened ever so slightly on her arm. "I'll only stay a few minutes, I promise."

Refusing him may incite him to more violence. I'd better do as he says. With her heart sinking, she walked up the steps and unlocked the front door. He managed to get inside before she did, so any last minute attempt to slam the door in his face was squelched. Once inside, he sat down on the couch in her living room. He started flipping through a magazine as if nothing had happened.

She wasn't sure what she should do. Her mouth was dry with fear. She reached down to pet Tubs, sitting by the rocking chair, but he sensed her fear. He immediately scampered downstairs to his hiding place in the basement. She perched on the edge of the rocking chair and continued her silent prayers: *Holy Mary, Mother of God, pray for me. Sweet Jesus, Lord God, please don't let him hurt me.*

Then she noticed the light on her phone machine was blinking. Since she and Thomas seemed to be playing a charade of normalcy, she decided to do what she would usually do under everyday circumstances. She hit the play button. She was startled to hear Tony's voice. He sounded worried.

"Francesca, it's me, Tony. If you're there, pick up the phone. I need to talk to you."

I *wonder what that's about. Maybe more news about Scotty.* Then she suddenly saw in her mind's eye a very sharp image of her husband's face. All her life, she had turned to special saints in times of desperate need. She was sure her beloved Dean was among the saints in heaven. *Dean, I really need you now. Please help me. Please tell me what to do.*

Thomas seemed to be getting agitated again. He had dropped the magazine and started pacing the floor. He must have read the worried expression on her face.

"Don't worry. I'm not going to hurt you. It's just that it's been hell having to conceal my feelings for Randall all this time."

She didn't say anything. She just nodded, so he'd keep on talking. *The longer he talks, the more time I have to figure out what to do. The longer he talks, the more chance that someone might show up at my door. Someone, anyone, please come to visit me.*

He raked his fingers through his hair in an agitated way. "I really loved him. I was in a relationship with a very nice woman when he started coming on to me." He paused. "Well, there's no need for any more secrecy. I might as well tell you her name since I've already told you so much. It was Lily. Does that surprise you?"

"Not really." She was trying to digest this piece of information. Of course, it all made sense in a sick sort of way.

"I wanted to change my ways. I wanted to settle down, get married to Lily, and have the house with the white picket fence. I was sick of the whole bisexual thing. I decided to go straight. Then Randall came along, and I fell for him in a big way."

He sat back down on the couch. He picked up a cushion and crushed it against him. "Well, then it really got messy. Randall and I became a pretty hot item, and I tried to hide it from Lily. But she found out and got very jealous. She told me in no uncertain terms to choose between her and him. And I chose him."

He nervously rolled up his sleeves as if he were too warm. Francesca noticed sadly that he had very big muscles.

"Before long, Randall started getting antsy. Now that I look back, I can see he was the kind of man who'd never commit to anyone. And he was feeling pressured by our relationship, so he started playing up to Lily. When I found out he was seeing her, I confronted him about it. He said he was through with me. He said he was going to go back to her and resume the marriage."

He laughed in a bitter way that sounded more like a cough. "I just couldn't take it anymore. I was totally obsessed with him. And I still loved him. So I wrote to him and practically begged him to come back to me."

Despite the warmth of the house, Francesca suddenly experienced an icy current that started in her toes and shot up to her scalp. *Did this man kill Randall? Am I sitting here in my living room with a killer*?

Thomas continued crushing the cushion in his strong hands. He wasn't looking at her now, just staring absently at the floor.

"I went over to see him after the choir party." His voice was a monotone.

"I decided to ask him, once and for all, if there was any chance of a serious commitment between us. But he just laughed at me." He clenched his fists at the memory, and threw the cushion savagely on the floor. "And that's what did it."

Francesca was feeling extremely cold now. *I've got to get out of here, but how?*

"I could have taken any reaction but that." His voice broke and he leaned over, cradling his head in his hands as he began sobbing.

She had to act quickly. She rushed across the room, pushed open the door, and started running across the front yard. *I'll pound on Myra's door for help,* she thought frantically. But it took only seconds for him to reach her and overpower her.

"Where the hell do you think you're going?" He gripped her wrists tightly. "I thought I could trust you." His voice had taken on a rough nasty tone, very different from the refined tone of voice he usually used.

The voice is familiar somehow, she thought.

"I told you I wouldn't hurt you." But of course he was doing just that. He was clutching her wrists so fiercely that he was stopping the circulation. She could feel the bruises starting.

Then she realized where she'd heard the voice before. "You're the one who threatened me on the phone, aren't you?"

"Yeah, I ran into Scotty near Randall's house and he said you were asking the old lady questions. I figured that call would discourage you. But you're very persistent, aren't you?"

She looked around frantically, hoping someone would come along and notice them, but she said nothing.

"Now just be a good girl and come inside, and we'll have some coffee." His voice assumed a placating tone, as if he were talking to a child.

"No!" she screamed. "Let me go! I'm not going back in!" But the more she struggled against him, the stronger he seemed to grow.

Where the hell are my neighbors? I'm never watching TV again. Someone could be killed right here on the front lawn and no one would ever hear a thing.

At that moment, a pair of yellowish eyes peered through the shrubbery that ran along the front of Francesca's house. When she saw the eyes, her first reaction was that it was some kind of apparition.

Then she realized who the eyes belonged to. Her neighbor's dog, Bainbridge. The big clumsy animal emerged silently from the shrubbery and appeared at her side.

"Get away, you mutt!" Thomas spat the words at the dog and gave him a quick kick. Then he started pulling Francesca roughly back toward the house.

She suddenly remembered Myra telling her about Bainbridge's hidden qualities. "Bainbridge, defend, defend!" she shouted.

Managing to free one of her hands, she pointed at Thomas in a way that the dog instantly recognized. Bainbridge didn't hesitate. Snarling and baring his teeth, he sprang for Thomas, knocking the man down and pinning him securely beneath the dog's muscular body.

* * *

Myra Findley turned the volume down on her TV. She was sure she had heard a noise outside. She peered out her front window and saw a very unusual gathering on Francesca's front lawn.

A man was flailing wildly beneath Bainbridge and yelling for dear life. Then she heard someone banging on her front door. She opened the door and saw Francesca standing there, crying hysterically: "Call the police!" Then she sank down on Myra's porch in a dead faint.

Seconds after Myra dialed the police station's number, a car pulled up outside, but it didn't have the flashing blue lights she had expected.

A man emerged from the car, running. As he ran, he pulled out his gun and pointed it at the other man, still struggling beneath the growling, snarling dog. Myra was now on her front porch, anxiously bending over Francesca and calling her name. She was relieved to find a strong pulse in her neighbor's wrist.

"Call him off, call him off!" Myra heard the man under her dog screaming. She quickly rushed over. "I'm Investigator Viscardi with Decatur Police," the man with the gun said to her.

"Should I call off my dog?" she asked quickly. He nodded.

"Excellent work, Bainbridge." Her voice was loud and firm. "You may stop now."

She was pleased to see how quickly her words broke the spell. Bainbridge immediately released his hold on the man and trotted to her side with his tail wagging.

* * *

"Get up," Tony growled at Thomas. "You're under arrest for the murder of Randall Ivy."

Tony didn't take his eyes off the bleeding man who was struggling to his feet just as two police cars, blue lights flashing, pulled up. As more officers rushed to the scene, Tony observed something he had seen a few times before in his many years in homicide. The prisoner snapped. Thomas broke down, sobbing, and had to be restrained by two of the policemen.

"You're right," he screamed, as the officers handcuffed Thomas and led him to the police car. As they put him in the back seat, Tony could hear Thomas shouting, “I killed Randall and I’m glad I did. He made my life a living hell.”

But Tony wasn’t listening. His only concern was Francesca. *If that guy hurt her, I don’t know what I’ll do.* He rushed over to the neighbor’s porch and crouched down beside Francesca as she started to regain consciousness. She looked at him in a dazed way.

“Everything is fine,” Tony whispered. “You’re safe.”

Francesca tried to smile, but it looked like her bruised mouth hurt too much. She tried to get up, but she was too weak. Tony lifted her to her feet.

“Are you alright? Did he hurt you? Do you need a doctor?”

As he helped her up, he noticed that a small crowd had gathered in the street, where the neighbor was answering their questions. Meanwhile, three small children were taking turns riding on the attack dog’s back.

Francesca seemed to be dizzy, so she leaned against him as he helped her into her house.

“Don’t need a doctor. Just bruises. And I’m so cold.”

* * *

When they got inside the house, Francesca collapsed on the couch and began shivering. Tony went into her bedroom and came back with a blanket and a quilt. He covered her up and then turned on the heat full blast. Then he went into the kitchen and she heard the ding of the microwave. When he returned, he handed her a glass of warm milk.

"Here, drink this, it will help relax you and warm you up," he said in the kindest tone of voice she'd heard in a long time.

She accepted the glass like a little child and sipped slowly, wincing as the rim touched her bruised lips. After he made a quick call to the police station, Tony sat beside her and cradled her in his arms.

"Now tell me what happened," he said tenderly.

She broke down then and started crying. She felt like a dam had burst in her heart. He held her until she could talk again. Then she told him about how Thomas had turned violent and how she had feared for her life.

"He and Randall were lovers," she whispered, taking another sip of the warm milk.

"And he killed Randall," Tony added.

She looked at him questioningly, wondering how he knew. He told her what he'd discovered about Thomas' criminal record.

"I was lucky," he said. "The officer who was dispatched that night to White's house remembered the party. He told me some of the partygoers were cross-dressers."

"You told me Mrs. Brumble claimed she saw two women visiting Randall the night he died. Well, I figured all along that Mrs. Brumble was confused, and the second woman was actually the first one – Patricia – who'd returned after going out to get something."

"Like a bottle of Scotch?"

"Exactly." He looked at her almost sheepishly. "I'm sorry for not taking your hunches more seriously at first. But I did eventually do some investigating on my own, even though the case was officially closed. And when I talked to Patricia a second time, unofficially, she told me that she and Randall had…er…had a brief interlude on the couch that night, but then she left afterwards -- and definitely didn't return until the next morning."

Francesca jumped when the phone rang. "My nerves are really frazzled."

"Not to worry. I'll get it."

She could tell by his comments that it was Myra, calling to check on her. After he hung up, he laughed. "She said, and I quote: 'You tell her that Bainbridge will be right here if anything else happens.'" Even Francesca chuckled when Tony added that he'd heard what sounded like an approving woof in the background.

Tony took a seat in the rocking chair. "Are you still awake enough to hear the ending of the story?"

Her eyes were growing heavy, but her curiosity was keeping her awake. "Yes, please go on."

"Well, then I stopped in to see Mrs. Brumble again. Even though I don't think she's the most reliable witness in the world, she insisted she had seen two different women that night. The first one I knew was Patricia. But she described the second one as shorter than Patricia."

He adjusted the quilt and stroked her head tenderly.

"That's when I ruled out Lily and Candy as candidates for being the second woman. Lily, Patricia, and Candy are about the same height."

He stopped for a moment and went into the kitchen, returning with a glass of water, which he handed to Francesca. She gratefully drained it.

"When I had supper with Lily tonight, I started wondering why she wanted those love letters so badly, especially if, as she claimed, she didn't write them herself. There had to be something in them, something about Randall, she wanted to hide."

He took the empty glasses into the kitchen and returned with a bag of ginger snaps. He opened the bag and offered it to her, and she took a handful of cookies and began eating them. She was starting to feel warm again – and safe.

"I think she desperately wanted to keep the truth from coming out about Randall," he said. "After all, she'd spent a lifetime protecting her daughter, and she didn't want to blow it. Lily was afraid of what was in the letters."

Francesca ate another cookie and offered the bag to him. "Are you falling asleep, darling?" he asked.

"No, please go on. I want to hear the rest."

"Well, when I discovered that White had hosted a party with a bunch of drag queens in attendance, I put together all the pieces. The second shorter 'woman' who visited Randall that night was really a man in drag. And it was this 'woman' – Thomas – who poisoned his ex-lover."

Francesca shuddered. *I could have been his second victim.*

He bent down and kissed her lightly on her cheek. She was very sleepy now, the stress and the warm milk taking their toll. Her muscles were crying out in pain from all the tension of the evening, and she could see purple bruises rising on her wrists and arms.

"You need to get some sleep, darling," he said softly.

"I'm really afraid to be here alone, Tony. Is there any chance you might call some of my friends to come and stay over?

"You got it." He went over to her phone book and, following her instructions, called Molly, Rebecca, and Shirley. She could hear him explaining what had happened, and could imagine their astonished reactions. It was only fifteen minutes later that the doorbell rang, and there was Molly. By this time, Francesca had washed her face with cold water, changed into pajamas, and climbed into bed.

She could hear Molly in the living room.

"So you're with the police? Well, listen, I need to ask you about a parking ticket I got last week while I was getting my hair done downtown. The meter was broken and I..."

Tony interrupted. "I'm with homicide. You'll want to contact someone at city hall about that."

A few moments later, Molly appeared in the bedroom. She gave Francesca three extra-strength aspirins, a glass of water, and a big kiss on the cheek.

"These will help you sleep and make your muscles relax a bit, so you won't be too sore in the morning."

"Yes, doctor."

Molly smiled. "Do you need anything else?"

"Tubs. He's probably hiding in the basement."

She heard voices in the living room again and then the sound of someone going down the stairs, and in a few seconds Molly entered her room, carrying Tubs.

"Here he is. He'll definitely keep you warm." Molly gently placed the purring cat beside Francesca on the bed. "Oh, Tony is getting ready to leave. He said to tell you goodnight."

Francesca heard the doorbell ring again and then the voices of Rebecca and Shirley. She could also hear Tony, evidently filling them in on what had happened. A few moments later, she saw Rebecca and Shirley standing in the doorway.

"Now don't worry about a thing," Shirley whispered. "We are spending the night here, and we'll make sure you're safe."

Rebecca added: "That's one good-looking police officer out there, girlfriend, and I have the feeling he's not just here on a professional call!"

As Francesca was falling asleep, she heard the front door open, and the sound of Tony leaving. She nestled against Tubs.

Thank you, God, for sparing my life. She was asleep in five minutes.

* * *

Waffles. That was Francesca's first thought the next morning when she awakened.

As she rolled over in bed, she noticed that every muscle in her body ached as if she had the flu. *But I'm alive, and I'm famished.*

Feeling like she was 100 years old, she slowly made her way to the bathroom and took a hot shower. *Forget the make-up.* She combed her hair and dressed. Then she glanced in the mirror and reconsidered. She decided on just a touch of lipstick, but when she tried to apply it, her lips were too sore.

When she walked into the dining room with Tubs at her heels, Tony was already there, reading the morning paper. She could hear Molly and Rebecca bustling around in the kitchen.

"Shirley had to leave early," Molly called out. "Her family can't survive long without her."

Tony stood up quickly when he saw her and took her tenderly in his arms. *He looks so nice,* Francesca thought, *I wish I'd spent more time getting ready.*

"How are you feeling?

"I feel like a truck ran over me." Her lips were making it difficult to enunciate clearly. "But I also have this feeling of utter exhilaration at being alive."

He gave her a hug. "I'm very glad you're alive too. How about some waffles?" He paused. "It's one of the few things I can make from scratch."

"Sounds heavenly." She sat down slowly on the chair. Muscles she hadn't realized existed were making their painful presence known.

Molly came into the room and handed her a mug of coffee. "Better today?" Francesca nodded gratefully and took a sip of coffee. A few minutes later, Tony placed a platter of waffles on the table, while Rebecca poured everyone orange juice.

"A man who can cook!" Molly put waffles on her plate. "You don't have a twin brother, by any chance?"

Francesca poured a generous stream of syrup over her waffles. "Not to change the subject, but there's still something I'm wondering about." She looked at Tony. "What about the bottle of Scotch?"

Molly and Rebecca looked up from their waffles.

"I think we'll discover when Thomas makes a full confession that he brought the Scotch over so he and Randall could have a few drinks together."

Tony paused from his waffles. "But Randall wasn't used to drinking the hard stuff and got thoroughly sloshed. Then they evidently had a big argument. Somewhere along the line, Randall or Thomas made a pot of coffee. Thomas saw the prescription bottle and figured the coffee would hide the taste."

Molly chimed in now. "But sleeping pills wouldn't dissolve fully in coffee, and even if he was drunk, wouldn't Randall have noticed them?"

Tony started refilling all their coffee cups. "Randall wasn't taking pills. His doctor had prescribed chlorohydrate, a liquid medication. It's often used by insomniacs who have trouble swallowing pills. So all Thomas had to do was put a big dose of the medication in the coffee. The coffee disguised the taste, and Randall was so drunk, it didn't take much."

Tony went into the kitchen, returning in a few minutes with another platter of steaming waffles. He passed them around to the three women and took a second helping for himself.

I like a man who can cook, Francesca thought. Her own skills in the kitchen were fairly limited, although she did have a few Italian recipes that turned out well.

"There are plenty more, so just enjoy," he said. After a few moments, Francesca put her fork down and gave the handsome man across the table from her a serious look.

"Tony, I hate to sound like someone in a soap opera, but I mean this sincerely. How can I ever thank you for coming to my rescue like that?"

Rebecca and Molly suddenly found something they just had to do in the kitchen, which left her alone with Tony.

He smiled. "Well, my dear, we'll think of something." He gave her an exaggerated wink that caused her to blush. "But it's really your neighbor's dog that saved the day, not me."

At that moment, Francesca glanced outside. There was Bainbridge busily depositing a pile of doggy manure on her lawn. She put down her fork and made her way slowly to the front door and opened it wide. Bainbridge sat on his haunches and gazed at her with his yellow eyes, evidently expecting a reproof.

His tail wagged excitedly when she called him over and presented him with his very own plate of crispy waffles.

CPSIA information can be obtained at www.ICGtesting.com
Printed in the USA
LVOW041145010212

266434LV00001B/24/P